Thora

A Spartan Hoplite's Slave

THORA

A SPARTAN HOPLITE'S SLAVE

by
Cameron North

WASP Publishing

WASP Publishing
Kennedyville, MD 21645
www.WASPpublishing.com

ISBN-13 (paperback):   978-1-7321153-5-4
ISBN-13 (ebook):   978-1-7321153-7-8

Second Edition – April 2019 – 1001.04

Credits
Editor: Randie J. Creamer
Editor: Shalini G.
Editor: Julia Vinson
Cover Design: May Dawney Designs

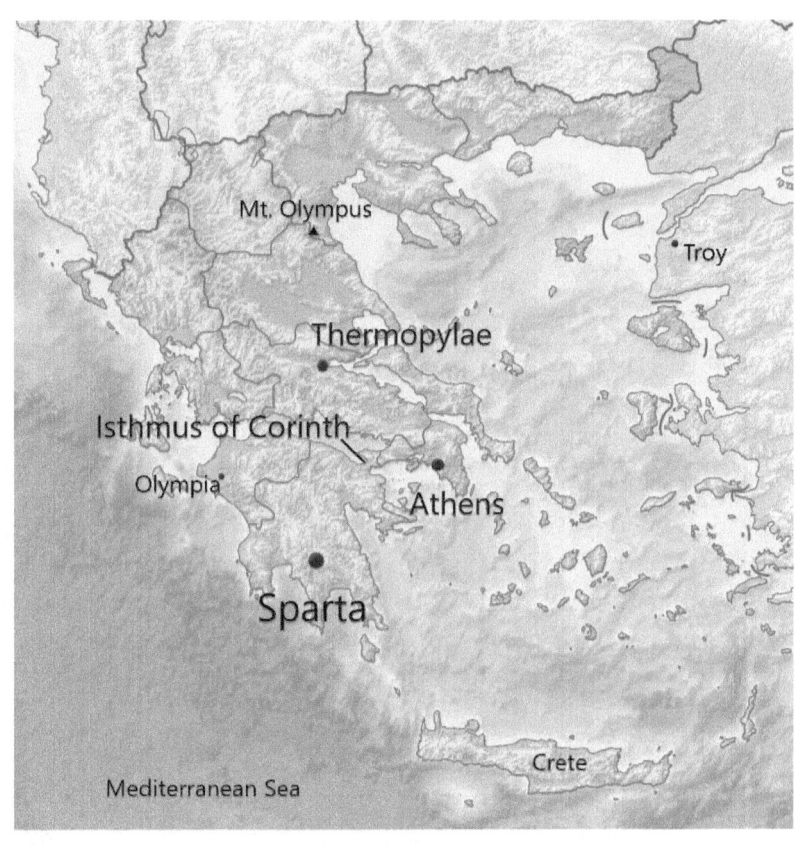

Map of Greece
Ca. 480 BC

Contents

PROLOGUE

pollo's burning yellow chariot hung in the western sky and continued riding across the arid summer sky. In the northern district of Sparta, a powerful woman weaved through the city's twisted streets until she came upon a villa. From the Greek symbol on the gate, she knew she was at the correct house. Through word of mouth, she had located a slave trader, who mainly sold to the Spartan *polis*. With a sidelong glance, she assured that her elder slave caught up to her.

The elder slave, Cesare, had trailed respectfully behind his owner. He paused several steps behind her and awaited their welcome into the slave trader's home. In recent years, Cesare had developed gray streaks through his dark hair, and his brown eyes were slightly cloudy. Time made his skin form soft rolls, and his shoulders fell forward rather than remain square. Cesare's speed in the house had become slower each year, and it already concerned his owner.

The Spartan woman gazed upon the courtyard beyond the gate's iron bars. She was pleased when a scraggly slave unlatched the bolt and allowed her to enter the villa. With a neutral gaze, she stole the chance to take in the slave trader's courtyard, which measured his wealthy stature in life.

The slave sealed the gate after Cesare joined his owner. He briefly bowed to them, then silently left.

It was a brief wait until a short and portly man in a soft blue *chiton* strolled out from one of the rooms. He had the same slave with him and ordered him to fetch the slaves for sale. "You are Halcyon." He continued crossing the courtyard to his guest. "Your husband, Euclid, mentioned you would be here today." He offered his hand.

"I am Halcyon."

"And I am Telamon." For a beat, Telamon lusted over the emerald eyes framed by dark, wavy hair that was held back by braids. He had heard gossip about Halcyon, the king's royal hoplite, who was known as the Iron Edge. He was enthralled by Halcyon's beauty. Even in her ornate lilac *peplos*, she was clearly built to fight. Her defined arms were perhaps sculpted by Ares. Her grip against his hand was powerful. Soft scars traced down her arms, and one was distinct across her collarbone. She was a living legend, Telamon knew.

"I am looking for a slave. One of mine died this past winter." Halcyon released the slave trader's meaty hand from their clasp. "I was informed you are the best source."

"Yes." Telamon stepped to his side and indicated the line of eight slaves behind him. "I have the finest slaves." He curiously studied Halcyon's beautiful necklace, which he assumed was a family heirloom.

Like Halcyon, there were a handful of secret clients in Sparta who purchased slaves. Many of the clients had amassed their private fortunes outside of Sparta's reach because commerce was illegal in the city and territories. The majority of the slaves were owned by the polis and were freely provided to the Spartans. Daily, common chores were for the slaves so that Spartans could strictly focus on the military. Even with so few slave owners, Telamon learned that his clients were extremely wealthy. Price was a short discussion in most transactions.

Halcyon approached the available slaves. She carefully studied each face. Three slaves were obviously foreigners, most likely brought in from war. "I require a cook."

Cesare shadowed his owner and also scanned the faces. Concern balled in his stomach because none looked terribly promising for the household. Like his owner, he wanted another, but younger, slave in the household. Many of his daily chores included upkeep of the home, courtyard, stable, horses, and surrounding lands, and Cesare was a terrible cook.

"A female cook." Halcyon turned to the slave trader.

Telamon pointed to the female slave near the end. "This one is a fine cook and Illyrian, but her Greek is strong."

Halcyon frowned. The indicated slave was weathered with time. "Far too old." Cesare was old enough, and adding another elder slave was concerning to Halcyon. "I need a young one." She studied the other available slaves.

Telamon pointed at the only young-looking, female slave in the lineup. "Glauce has not learned to cook, but she is excellent at weaving."

Halcyon was further displeased by the news. Cesare could easily teach weaving to the next slave. She considered leaving Telamon's residence, as it appeared he had no young slave to suit her needs.

"Perhaps you could purchase both slaves." Telamon smiled at the brilliant idea. "The elder can teach the girl to cook." He could sell two of them and double his profits. He was about to speak again when he noticed Halcyon had left his side.

Halcyon had slowed when she neared an unusual young woman, who was crouched by the plants with a water *oinochoe*. As the slave stood up, her long legs seemed to never end. Her pale features were framed by golden waves of hair. Halcyon was truly fascinated by her.

Telamon shuffled over and stiffened at what slave captivated his client.

"How much for her?"

Telamon shook his head and rested his linked hands on his rotund belly. "She is not for sale."

"How much?" Halcyon demanded. She had yet to tear her gaze away from the slave. At first, it had been the sunny hair that captured Halcyon's attention.

"You may purchase any but her." Telamon prized this slave — a breathing trophy in his household.

Halcyon was lost in her admiration and wondered if the sky had been softly blown into the slave's eyes by the gods. She glared at Telamon and tested him with an offer. "A hundred *drachmas*."

Telamon balked at the weak offer, willing to kill the slave before he accepted such a low price.

"Three hundred drachmas." Halcyon had read his disgust in the earlier offer, but his current hesitation was promising to her.

"She is untrained. She is quite the Cerberus, stubborn and troublesome."

Halcyon's lips pulled into a small grin at the slave being compared to Hades's three-headed dog. With a deep stare, she saw the storm inside the golden-haired woman. Still, even a defiant and rare slave could fall into the polis's heavy hands. "Four hundred drachmas."

Telamon played with the gold signet ring on his pinky. He narrowed his gaze at the slave. She was indeed a Cerberus in his household. "She speaks little Greek."

Halcyon considered whether Telamon was truly trying to discourage her or discourage himself. She refused defeat, like any hoplite, and now had to own the unique slave. In Telamon's hands, the slave would suffer, then eventually be given to the polis when he tired of her. She would certainly die as a *helot*. Halcyon could see the beautiful fire that burned in her spirit. "Five hundred drachmas." She turned to Telamon. "And I will purchase another slave in two to three months."

For a long moment, Telamon warred with himself. He had paid half that amount to acquire her from another slave trader, who found her to be too much trouble. He was doubling his money and was guaranteed another sale too. Telamon sighed and held out his hand. "I accept."

Halcyon clasped his arm in final agreement.

"She does cook," Telamon said after the shake.

Reaching between her peplos, Halcyon fished out a pouch. "There are ten owls." She handed the coins to him. "The rest will be brought to you by tomorrow's sunset."

Telamon's mouth watered at the hefty weight of the ten silver dekadrachm in his hands. Rumors were that Halcyon had history in Athens if she was using their coin, which had Athena's owl stamped on it. He was grateful she had them on hand because he worried about being paid with Sparta's worthless iron disc.

Halcyon turned to Cesare. "See to her."

"Yes, *éra*." Cesare bowed his head to his owner, then neared the tall slave.

Telamon signaled his same scraggly slave to help organize the sold slave. He doubted she had many possessions, if any. He then escorted Halcyon back to the gate.

"Tell me her history."

Cradling the pouch in his hands, Telamon paused beside the black gate and said, "I purchased her from an Athenian slaver some time ago. Like myself, he had trouble training her. He received her as a payment from a Phoenician merchant." He paused, then mentioned, "I believe she is from Gaul."

Halcyon considered the information for a moment. People from Gaul lived in the northern lands that the Romans found of interest. "Her age?" she asked.

"Perhaps twenty or so." Telamon weakly shrugged. "She is in her prime." He unlatched the gate.

"Her name, Telamon?"

Telamon glanced at the approaching slaves. He studied the tall, sunny-haired slave, who was now Halcyon's problem. "Makistia."

Frowning, Halcyon knew it was a slave's name, which meant "tallest" in Greek. Most likely, Telamon knew nothing about the slave's birth name, but perhaps she could learn it in time.

ᐸHAᐣTᕮR ONᕮ

Makistia was startled awake by a bang at the door. A fortnight had passed since Makistia joined Halcyon's house and had yet to adjust to the early mornings. Rushing to the door, she opened it a crack until she made out the elder slave's face.

"It is time to begin," Cesare told her. "Meet me downstairs." He disregarded the fact that Makistia barely knew Greek, but she understood him well enough. Cesare hurried off without another word or look.

With a frown, Makistia shut the door, leaned her back against it, and stared at her tiny, square confines. The walls were bright, like snow from her homelands. Only a single window broke up the whitewashed interior. Currently, a mat blocked the night's cooler air. On the floor, a bedroll and a ruffled fur blanket called to her. But Makistia had to prepare for the day, although Apollo had yet to mount his chariot and draw the sun over the eastern horizon.

On the first day, Makistia had received a detailed tour of the two-story villa. She had been impressed by Halcyon's home and lands, which stood on the eastern side of the Greek city at the end of a torturous street. Like many Greek homes, it was made from a combination of wood, stone, and clay. A classic rustic tile had been used on the roof. When visitors arrived, they entered through the front gate and were greeted by a beautiful courtyard with a fountain, draping plants from the second floor, and a marble bench.

There were two floors to the home that divided work from pleasure. The downstairs had several important rooms for supplies, bathing, and weaving or potting. Additionally, the kitchen was tucked into the rear and was accessible from the outside as well as from the courtyard. The most important room, however, was the husband's own social room. The upstairs had several living quarters for slaves, guests, and the masters. One room upstairs was dedicated for the wife's use, but Halcyon was rarely seen in it. Makistia wondered about her owner's constantly missing presence in the house. Most women in Athens were tied to their homes, but not Halcyon.

Beyond the villa, the lands were vast. Directly beside the house was a stable with twelve stalls for Halcyon's horses. Alongside the stable was an open grassy field, but Makistia noticed strange wood posts. She was unsure of their purpose.

Farther beyond the open grasses was a rolling field that the polis farmed with helots.

Initially, Makistia spent most of her time at the stable, cleaning the stalls. The task was arduous, even for her. She was accustomed to constant labor, but the stable's needs were beyond the normal. Much of her time was spent mucking stall after stall. Each day began in stench and ended in soreness. As soon as a job was done, she was required to repeat it. Makistia decided the labor was meant to break her thunderous spirit. She resolved to play by the owner's rules, for now.

Shortly, Makistia found Cesare and was shown the kitchen in detail. Before sun high, Cesare took Makistia to the *agora* where she would need to go nearly every day for supplies. Makistia tried keeping track of the lengthy list of items. Most days would require food for the house and, occasionally, textiles for clothing, reeds for weaving baskets, or clay to make new pots. Cesare insisted he would handle the supplies for the stable, which relieved Makistia.

Cesare had conversations with the merchants and pointed at Makistia several times. The merchants smiled and nodded at her. It was obvious they were informed about her lack of the Greek tongue. They seemed too curious about her rare features, which Makistia had become accustomed to since she was torn from her homelands.

After the agora, Makistia helped Cesare with the goods for the day and returned home. Makistia expected to see Halcyon at some point. She had only seen her on the first day, but since then, Halcyon had been elusive.

Cesare showed her where the different foods went in the supply room and the kitchen. Then they started prepping for the midday meal. She sensed that Cesare was curious about her skills in the kitchen. Perhaps he expected her to make something more from her homelands than a classic Greek dish. Recently, Makistia had learned many traditional Greek meals due to her time in Athens.

Cesare was obviously pleased with Makistia's skills in the kitchen. Together, they carried the tray of food, an oinochoe full of wine, and a *skyphos* through the house. They located Halcyon enjoying the sunlight in the courtyard. As a team, they quickly organized the meal on a table, then stepped aside and waited for any orders.

Halcyon finished reading a scroll about recent politics and slowly rolled it up. Her mind was on today's duty as the king's guard but pushed it away. She set the scroll on the bench to her left, then stood and went to the table. She was pleased by the spread of food. Briefly, her green eyes leveled on the tall slave whom she had acquired a fortnight ago.

"Is this her first attempt?" Halcyon asked Cesare.

Cesare kept his hands behind his back. "Yes, ĕra." Like his owner, he was surprised by Makistia's culinary skill. He hoped the taste pleased Halcyon, or else they would have taken a large step backward in finding an adequate new slave.

Halcyon slid into the stone seat at the round table. She had yet to allow Makistia to cook for her, finding it more important to hammer her expectations into Makistia. Normally, it would have only taken three to five days, but Makistia was a proud slave. Halcyon remedied Makistia's pride with long days of mucking the stable and farming with the helots. Her method seemed to temper the slave, at least for now.

A slight grin pulled at the corner of Halcyon's lips once she noted the heavy use of olives in the two dishes. It had an Athenian flare to it rather than a Spartan style. Halcyon made a mental note to have Cesare show Makistia what exactly made up a Spartan diet. But first, she tasted the dishes one by one and ate some of the bread. Overall, the meal's flavor was pleasing and happily settled with Halcyon.

Cesare shifted in his boots as he waited for Halcyon's thoughts.

"Cesare, excuse us." Halcyon peered up from the food and watched him leave.

Remaining still, Makistia wondered what Halcyon wanted from her, as they could hardly speak in a common tongue.

Halcyon tore a piece of bread and enjoyed its hearty texture. After swallowing, she cleared her throat and focused on Makistia. "We can only exchange a few words."

Makistia held her owner's gaze, unsure what was said to her.

"I plan to learn about you," Halcyon said, calmly. She raised an eyebrow, and curiosity colored her features. "I want to know who you are and where you come from."

Sighing, Makistia disliked that Greeks spoke to her regardless of the barrier.

"And I will find out." Halcyon picked up a wine skyphos that Cesare had filled earlier. She rested the clay skyphos in her lap. "First, you can tell me your name." She raised the skyphos to her lips and sipped the sweet wine.

Makistia clenched her hands behind her back. Halcyon's eyes held expectations that were lost on her.

Halcyon set the skyphos on the table. After a thought, she placed her hand against her chest and said, "My name is Halcyon." Then her hand traveled to Makistia's arm. "Your name is?"

Makistia narrowed her eyes at Halcyon. It was clear that Halcyon was asking her something, but she failed to translate the request.

Halcyon gave a soft sigh, stood up, and approached her. Again, she rested her hand on her own chest. "Halcyon." Then she touched Makistia's shoulder.

Briefly looking at the hand on her shoulder, Makistia studied Halcyon's cool features again and finally stated, "Makistia."

Halcyon shook her head in disapproval. "Your birth name." She narrowed her eyes and added, "Makistia is your slave name."

Makistia had a thin furrow across her brow. For some reason, her reply was insufficient even though it was true. Then it occurred to Makistia that her owner wanted her name by birth, from her homelands. She focused on her owner's waiting look.

"Thora," Makistia stated, her voice tinged with dignity. She was rewarded with a thin smile.

"Th-or-ah," Halcyon said disjointedly and released her. Makistia's real name was from faraway lands and completely foreign to Halcyon.

Makistia shook her head and slowly drew out her name. "Ttthhhooorrraaa." From Halcyon's expression, Makistia repeated it slower. "Th-or-a."

Halcyon was confused by the first two letters, attempting it again. "Thhhoraaa." After Makistia's nod, she tried it again at normal pace. "Thora."

Makistia had a small smile and nodded. "Yes," she agreed in Greek tongue. It was obvious that her owner was pleased to learn her birth name.

Returning to her seat, Halcyon nodded to herself and ordered, "Go see Cesare."

Makistia, or rather rightly called Thora, dipped her head and then quietly left her owner.

Halcyon had a grape between her index finger and thumb. As she studied it, she considered her new slave's birth name. It was rather special, just like Thora. Halcyon wondered what the name meant in Thora's native tongue.

Halcyon was content to forget the name Makistia.

* * *

Over the days, the sun tirelessly trekked across the sky. Gradually, the new slave adapted more to her surroundings. Her beginnings had been difficult, but she learned to respect her new owner. The first blossom of understanding budded when Halcyon learned Thora's birth name. However, Thora's bottled pride and Halcyon's will were still as Greek fire.

Eventually, Thora learned that Halcyon's constant absence was due to her duty as a warrior. Or rather a hoplite, Thora mentally corrected. A few times, Thora caught glimpses of Halcyon leaving through the gate in the soft dawn light with reflective armor. On occasions, Halcyon left at sunset to carry out her duty. But Thora always saw Halcyon for the evening meal.

One day, Thora was especially busy. She had risen earlier than normal in order to be prepared for this evening's event, which included a regular guest. By now, she should have been accustomed to her owner's special guest, who was excessively snobbish. Halcyon wanted the evening handled in a particular way. Thora clamped down on her frustration over the situation.

Thora sighed but continued slicing the flatbread. Her wandering thoughts disrupted her ˌfocus, and the knife unexpectedly ran down her thumb. She cursed and dropped the knife. After inspecting her bleeding thumb, she clamped down tightly on the wound with the towel from her *girdle*.

Cesare entered with a flustered expression. "Thora, hurry!" With an overbearing wake, he pointed at the partially cut bread but paused upon seeing Thora clutching her hand.

Once at her side, he tried inspecting her hand for the problem, but she kept refusing him. Annoyed because he wanted to help, Cesare swatted Thora's hand away. "Stop."

Thora followed the command from her superior and lowered her uninjured hand to her side.

Cesare was grateful and removed the towel, only to sigh at the minor cut. Ripping a piece of towel, he tied it over the bleeding wound, then handed her the towel while pointing at the bread again. "Hurry."

Thora nodded and returned to her task. She saw Cesare picking up a filled wine oinochoe from the counter and heading out of the kitchen. She stilled her knife and called, "Cesare?"

Cesare paused next to the entrance.

"Thank... you."

For once, Cesare traded a smile and then dashed out of the kitchen without another word.

Soon Thora placed the cut flatbread onto a wooden board. The board already held a large bowl of herbed olive oil, feta, and another bowl of grapes. She hoisted the substantial board off the counter, then left the kitchen.

Thora entered the courtyard, then turned to her right and climbed a small flight of steps. The upstairs had a small social room known as the *gynaikeion* that was reserved for the wife. Spartans continued many Greek traditions, despite the fact that Spartan women held full control of the house because their husbands were often in the barracks or at war. Thora thought the Greek home's segregation was strange compared to her homelands.

Thora hurried into the gynaikeion and found Cesare pouring wine for the guest. She wondered if Cesare knew of her disdain for the person.

Halcyon was pleased by Thora's arrival. "Thora," she said and pointed at her guest, who was sprawled out on a comfortable *kline*.

Thora understood and barely withheld her sigh. She went over and lowered the tray while the guest took her time selecting the food. Thora's patience was strained by her growing irritation.

The guest dipped a piece of flatbread in the oil and chomped down on it. "When does Euclid return home from the barracks?"

Halcyon finished sipping her sweet wine then lowered the skyphos onto the kline's soft linen. "Not for another month, Selene." Her fingers tangled in one of the skyphos's handles.

Selene chuckled and dipped her bread again. "Pity for him," she said, casually.

Halcyon grinned, not at the joke, but at the desire in Selene's eyes.

Selene took a few pieces of feta, and then she waved at Thora to leave her.

Thora crossed over to Halcyon and lowered the tray.

After eating a piece of feta, Halcyon freed a vine of grapes from the bowl. She peered up at Thora and pointed to the low table that was between her and Selene.

Bowing her head, Thora moved to the table to put down the board, then joined Cesare, who stood by the door with a beautiful clay oinochoe in his hands.

Selene considered the strange slave. "The barbar seems to have improved." Her insult about Thora's status as a barbarian was not lost on any.

"The stables appear to have helped her disposition."

Selene heartily laughed at Halcyon. "Your training is always effective." There was dark amusement in her eyes.

"I have been well taught," Halcyon said. She thought of her father, who was once an Athenaeum. He had moved his daughter, his ailing wife, and his fortunes to Sparta. In his late life, he taught Halcyon how to train slaves.

"Yes," Selene said. "Only the champion of the Heraea Games could do such."

Halcyon's eyes slotted at the mention of the games. She crossed her legs, which caused the slit in her chiton to reveal muscular calves. "The Heraea Games were child's play."

Selene softly laughed and said, "Perhaps to you, but many women struggle in those games."

"We fare well in those games."

"Maybe one day, you will find yourself in Olympia." Selene's grin was wide.

Halcyon remained neutral although she inwardly seethed at the mention of the games. In less than a month, the city of Sparta would send their most celebrated competitors to the seventy-fifth games in Olympia. However, Halcyon would be forbidden to enter the Olympics simply due to her gender. Not even her fame as the Iron Edge was enough to change the games' rules. Yet it was public knowledge that Halcyon sent her finest horses to the chariot games in Olympia and profited from the wins.

After a heavy sigh, Halcyon said, "Not even upon the death of Zeus would they allow women to compete."

Selene wagged an index finger. "Never doubt your fate."

Halcyon dismissed Selene's opinion.

Selene sobered after a curious thought. "When do you return to the barrack?"

"A little more than a fortnight," Halcyon replied. She was grateful it was on the very same day that the games started in Olympia. She needed the distraction.

"King Leonidas speaks highly of you." Selene dreamily pictured Halcyon in her bronze armor. She lost her smile and asked, "Have you been successful in seeking out a translator?"

Halcyon sipped her wine first. "I have found one who may assist me. He is due to arrive from Athens any day now."

Selene considered this further. "It seems an awful waste of coin to hire him just so he can teach your helot to speak our native tongue." She had learned that Halcyon had coin stored away from her father's inheritance. Such wealth in Sparta was rare.

Halcyon tilted her head at Selene. "Indeed." She set down her wine and plucked several grapes from the food board. "I am curious to learn her history." She had kept Thora's purchase private and allowed Selene to assume Thora was owned by the polis.

"She is a helot," Selene said, almost bitterly. "What matters is that she is skilled enough to cook decently."

Halcyon remained silent and waved Cesare over for a wine refill. After he approached, she held out a hand to the food. "Eat, Selene. Do not let my feta go waste."

Selene obliged and took a handful of the feta cubes. She curled back up on the kline.

Halcyon smiled and asked, "Can you stay tonight, Selene?"

Selene revealed a wicked grin at the invitation. "Of course." She enjoyed the glint in Halcyon's green eyes. It rekindled the heat low in her belly and the wetness between her legs.

Halcyon turned to the slaves. "Cesare, see that Thora begins preparing our meal."

"Yes, ĕra." Cesare bowed, grabbed Thora's wrist, and left with her. In the kitchen, he assisted Thora with making the meal.

Later, Thora returned to the gynaikeion and served Selene and then Halcyon. She placed the empty tray by the wooden board that was nearly barren. She went near the door, turned, and pressed her back against the wall.

Tonight was only the second time that Thora helped Cesare serve Halcyon and Selene together. Over the month, Thora had seen and heard Selene from a distance. She was not impressed by Selene. However, Thora tried to remain neutral toward Selene, who was important to Halcyon.

Thora openly observed the pair while they were immersed in their dinner and chatter. She first watched

Halcyon, who was much more dignified in her dining form. Over the years, Thora had actually picked up a few techniques of proper Greek dining etiquette by studying her owners. Then there was Selene, whom Thora had secretly nicknamed Linnr in her own tongue. Like the linnr in her homelands, Selene was a monster that slithered and hissed often at her.

Thora had grown to dislike Linnr. Mutually, Selene held no respect for Thora, a slave and a barbarian. Selene questioned why Halcyon had chosen the slave when there were more capable helots available from the polis. At least the beastly slave was Halcyon's problem, Selene thought.

With a careful eye, Thora assessed Selene, who was short compared to Thora. Selene's eyes were a dark brown and were nearly lost by her mammoth nose. Her hair was a classic mousy color with tight wavy locks. She often wore her hair up in a bun with a few curly strands falling about her shoulders and nape. Typically, Selene wore the same white chiton, but Thora imagined she owned more than one set. Selene was close to Thora's age, unmarried, and seeking a husband.

The traditions were different in Sparta than in Athens. The Athenian women married in their fifteenth year. The Spartan women wed closer to eighteen or even as late as twenty-two. Thora recalled being married shortly after her sixteenth birthday. She pushed away her old memories of home and her husband after Halcyon called her. She hastened and collected the empty plates.

"What a daydreamer," Selene said accusingly. "I cannot imagine what her barbaric mind is thinking up." She stared coldly up at Thora when she came to collect the empty plate from the table.

Sensing Selene's judgmental stare, Thora ignored it while collecting the dirty plates. Once gone from the room, she released a sigh and went to the kitchen to rid of the dishes in the wash tub. In a hurry, the strange but sweet dessert was organized, and Thora left with it and a full oinochoe.

When Thora returned to the suite, she placed the cut *gastrin* dessert onto the table and filled both the freewomen's skyphoi. Eventually, she returned to her quiet spot by the door and watched the women dine. The food's smells were making her stomach gently rumble, but memories from her homelands helped divert her attention.

"Thora!"

Thora jumped from Halcyon's shout and hastened to fill her and Selene's empty skyphoi.

"Perhaps she requires another punishment to get her out of her daydreams." Selene's gaze went cold as it lifted to Thora.

Curbing her annoyance, Thora finished pouring and grabbed the dessert plate before leaving the suite.

The freewomen continued talking, and the wine soaked through their resolve. At some point, while Thora was gone, Halcyon had moved to the kline beside her upright guest.

Thora entered the room with her refilled oinochoe. Cesare joined her but on the other side of the doorway.

Selene laughed at something, set her skyphos on the table, and placed her left hand on Halcyon's knee. "I cannot imagine."

Halcyon moved her skyphos away from her lips and revealed a grin. "Hopefully, I will never upstage my husband, though, in such a manner." She had already outranked her husband as a *hippeus*, an elite guard to the king, while Euclid continued as a low-ranking hoplite in the army.

Selene rolled her eyes. "How the people would talk. A husband's wife bested him in fair combat."

"I am not sure it would boast well in the barracks."

Selene shook her head. "I hear the men talk about you… the tales about the Iron Edge. They say the kings, especially King Leonidas, are fascinated by you." She leaned into the older woman. "I cannot blame them."

"Seleeene," Halcyon drew out. She set her skyphos down beside the other one. "This will not be going on for much longer."

Selene frowned, but it changed into a grin. "Yes, soon I will be the wife seeking the affections of a young maiden." She chuckled at her lover's seductive smile.

"I pray yours is as fine as mine has been," Halcyon said huskily. She leaned down to Selene.

Selene touched Halcyon's left cheek, then her lips met the soft ones above hers. Her eyes closed, and she enjoyed the long kiss.

Thora lowered her head when she saw the women kiss, but an excited heat started on her face, and she chided herself for it. Rarely did women show such affection in Thora's homelands compared to Spartan traditions.

Cesare was hardly embarrassed by Halcyon's romance with Selene. He was born and raised in the Greek culture. He was Greek himself, even if he was sold into slavery by his father.

Selene smiled at the end of the sensuous kiss and picked up her skyphos. "Thora?" She smirked at Thora's bowed head.

Thora neared Selene and tilted the clay oinochoe over Linnr's skyphos.

Halcyon openly assessed Thora, appreciating Thora's rare beauty. Selene caught Halcyon's interest in the beautiful slave, which turned her stomach. She suddenly leaned in for another warm kiss.

Thora clenched her teeth at the purposeful kiss. With a spark of defiance, she moved the tipped oinochoe forward until the red wine spilled all over a white lap.

Selene jerked out of the kiss and yelled, "By the gods!" The chilled liquid soaked through her lap. She stood up with the overflowing skyphos splashing over her chest.

Thora stepped back with a satisfied smirk.

Halcyon jumped to her feet. After a glance at Selene, she narrowed her eyes at Thora. Halcyon's features hardened, and she turned to Cesare. "Get some rags!"

Cesare had neared the group earlier, but he rushed out to handle the request.

Halcyon stepped around her cursing guest and approached Thora. She was shorter than Thora, yet her muscular build and raised anger made her powerful.

Selene turned her ire on Thora. "She purposely did that." She started coming after Thora.

Halcyon halted Selene. "She is my slave. Now sit."

Selene froze and saw the fire behind those green eyes. She sank down on the kline and waited for Cesare.

Halcyon centered her fury on Thora, who held her ground. Thora's blue eyes stormed with defiance.

There was no warning as a sickening smack echoed in the room. Thora went down from the sheer power in the slap. The clay oinochoe broke, and wine washed over the floor. Thora blinked back the natural sting in her eyes. She sharply inhaled the sweet scent of the wine, which reminded her why she was struck in the first place.

Halcyon bared her teeth at her fallen slave. She observed Thora touching her red cheek. Her eyes flickered to the clay pieces and the red wine over the floor. When Thora met her gaze, Halcyon saw the passionate fire in Thora that reminded her of herself as a hoplite. She turned to Cesare, who was shocked by her rare punitive demonstration. "Clean up the mess, Cesare, and remove her."

"Yes, ĕra." Cesare refocused, went around the kline, and came to Thora's side. It was rare that Halcyon ever harmed her slaves and preferred punishment over violence. He sympathized with Thora but suspected additional punishment would follow tomorrow, if not tonight. He cleaned the mess with his rags and helped Thora to her feet, hastening her out of the room before anything else happened.

Selene was stiff from the dampness. She looked as if she had been attacked and had bled on her chiton.

"I apologize, Selene." Halcyon returned to her spot on the kline with Selene. "It is obvious that she still requires a heavy hand." Later, she would consider what caused Thora's unexpected actions.

"Let us forget it now." Selene hoped she could ease Halcyon's temper, which was even fearful to Selene. "Besides, I will soon be out of my chiton."

"Yes." Halcyon leaned in for a kiss. She withdrew and said, "Shall we move to the bedroom now?"

Selene grazed Halcyon's cheek with the back of her hand. For a year, Halcyon had been her lover. "Yes, Halcyon. I am yours tonight."

CHAPTER TWO

Taking a break from the punishment, Thora leaned heavily against the pitchfork in her hands scowled at the stinky stall. Last night had ended badly after Thora had dumped wine on her owner's lover. Thora had been struck by Halcyon for the error. Her punishment had begun last night with no rest. To Thora, the horse manure was a more welcome smell than the *ouranē*. The ouranē were full of human waste that still made Thora nauseous. Several other straining chores were given to her until first light when she was sent to the stable.

After a step, Thora leaned against a post and wiped the sweat off her brow. She kept the pitchfork away from her face, arm stretched out in front of her. After the short break, she resumed mucking the horse's stall. The stable was about halfway done. When it was finished, she would resume her normal chores, which would be a relief.

Due to her weariness, Thora barely registered the footsteps in the stable before she felt the movement directly behind her. She was startled, spinning around with the pitchfork. Her fighting senses were ready, especially against the bronze-covered intruder.

"Calm down." Halcyon's voice rumbled behind the bronze helmet, the red plume on top making her even taller. Her right hand rested on a sword hilt. She was fully armored for her rotational day as a royal guard to the king.

Thora lowered the pitchfork after she recognized her owner under the armor and leaned it against a wall. For the first time, she was dazzled by the rich green orbs that glowed under the shiny helmet. Halcyon reached up and removed her helmet, the cheek plates gently brushing her temples.

Stepping back, Thora put space between her and Halcyon. Her eyes darted down to the sheathed *xiphos* at Halcyon's side. She parted her lips, but her foreign words hung silent on her tongue. In her culture, it was common practice for a woman to know enough about weapons that she could defend herself and her children. Some women even became warriors. However, in Greece, Thora doubted women knew how to even hold a kitchen knife. She thought perhaps it was illegal for a woman to wield a weapon or wear armor, but it appeared to be legal in Sparta.

Stretching out her hand, Halcyon brushed her fingertips across Thora's slightly bruised cheek. Thora flinched but in hurt pride rather than pain. She kept her eyes trained on her owner. Defiance once again stormed brightly in her eyes.

Halcyon slipped her fingertips under Thora's chin. She and Thora silently spoke their emotions through their locked gazes. Even without a common tongue, Halcyon and Thora were able to convey their wills. Halcyon was truly displeased and insulted by Thora's actions last night, especially after she believed they had found a common ground. She had been wrong.

Thora hardly regretted her actions last night. In her homelands, Thora would have done the same to any woman or man who scorned her like Selene. Although Thora was a slave in Greece, her mind and spirit were still that of a freewoman.

Halcyon released a frustrated breath after she realized that breaking Thora's pride would be comparable to traversing Hades. She had hoped to work out an agreement with Thora, who refused to be tamed like other slaves. Their mutual respect would have to be rebuilt.

As a peace offering, Halcyon held out the bronze helmet from under her arm. Earlier she had noted Thora's fascination with her uniform.

Gazing down, Thora accepted the helmet, turning and inspecting every part of its shiny surface, then running her fingers through the red plume. The helmet had once been a perfect piece from the smith, but it had since collected wounds from fights, battles, and maybe even wars. A faint dent on the once smooth top caught Thora's eyes. Several times, she ran her fingertip over various scratches, especially one heavy gouge over the right temple. Her fingernail passed through it, and she imagined it was from a sword blade. From the front, Thora admired the craftsmanship details given to the eye slits, nose guard, and the fine metal etching that followed the helmet's edge line all the way around to the back.

Thora returned the helmet and grew bold about the rest of her owner's uniform. For a beat, she glanced at the xiphos's hilt, and unknowingly, she stretched out her hand to touch it. Suddenly, her wrist was hooked, and it halted her movements. Thora's attention snapped to her owner.

"No." Halcyon redirected Thora's hand to rest on her bronze cuirass that went down to her lower waist. She set Thora's hand against her bronze clad stomach. "Yes." She then lifted Thora's hand and placed it against her helmet. "Yes." She pointed at her bronze greaves and nodded. She lastly placed Thora's hand near the xiphos's hilt. "No."

Thora's hand was freed after the simple instructions. She took the earlier invitation to the cuirass and touched the stomach area. It was firm and warm, like the helmet. There were ribbed spots that mimicked muscles and a belly button. Higher up, the cuirass was specially crafted for Halcyon's upper body, including a pair of nipples that matched her male counterparts' cuirasses. At the top, two small, bronze rings allowed for the red cape to be hooked to them. Again, Thora was impressed by the craftsmanship and even the fact that a smith would accommodate a female. It was plainly obvious that her owner was held in high esteem by her male counterparts.

Tilting her head, Halcyon watched Thora explore her armor. It was the first time she had adorned herself in her armor in front of her new slave. She wondered how common it was for women in Thora's homelands to wear armor and wield a sword. Halcyon secretly enjoyed Thora's keen interest in her hoplite uniform. Spartan women looked the other way, but Thora was transfixed by her.

Thora withdrew her hand after she released one of the decorative leather straps that was attached to the base of the cuirass. She lifted her blue eyes to Halcyon, silently conveying that she was done.

Halcyon studied Thora, and her mind skipped back to last night. She pictured Thora pouring the wine into Selene's lap. Halcyon's rage had since cooled from last night. She shook her head and asked, "What were you thinking, Thora?"

Thora frowned at the words, but she suspected the topic. "Selene?" she asked. She was unsure if she was allowed to speak Linnr's proper name. Yet she hardly cared if it was impolite, because Linnr was ill-mannered.

"Yes, Selene."

Thora quickly caught on to what bewildered her owner. Her annoyed expression grew as she thought more about the obnoxious freewoman, who often bedded Halcyon. "Selene ist ein linnr." After Halcyon shook her head, Thora sighed and ran her fingers through her long, straight hair as she considered how to explain it. She stared at the dirt under her feet as she pictured a linnr, then she straightened up. She hastily grabbed her pitchfork from the wall.

Halcyon tensed until she realized Thora's intent with the pitchfork.

Thora was hardly an artist, but she drew a linnr in the dirt. Its long serpent body told most of its origin and Thora's meaning behind the nickname. Halcyon bent over and studied the childlike image scratched into the dirt. She was perplexed, so she looked at Thora, who pointed at the picture. "Selene." For emphasis, she hissed in example. "Selene... linnr." Perhaps it was in poor taste to explain a linnr, due to the simple fact that Thora was depicting Halcyon's lover as such a wretched creature.

Halcyon's jaw snapped shut, and she realized what was in front of her. It was quite similar to a snake. Everything aligned, then she turned to Thora. "Lenrm?"

Thora shook her head then slowly pronounced, "Linnr."

"Linnr," Halcyon said perfectly.

"*Já*," Thora agreed. She set the pitchfork aside again.

Halcyon stared at the drawing, then slowly met Thora's smiling features. She raised a dark eyebrow and pointed at the Linnr. "Selene?"

Thora's smile faded against her owner's stern features. She dipped her head in silent confirmation.

Halcyon remained stoic. She realized the first foreign word she learned was about her lover, which was anything but complimentary. While studying the drawing, Halcyon considered her options.

Thora fisted her right hand at her side and waited for a physical response from her owner, who could be volatile without warning. Thora lifted her chin and prepared for Halcyon's reaction, but she held her ground to the short yet powerful freewoman.

Halcyon kept her head down as she lifted her helmet. She slid it on and allowed it to cover her face. Her eyes pierced through the darkness of the helmet's slits once she lifted her head. She said nothing and turned on her heels. Her red cape floated behind her as she exited the stable. Thankfully, she held down her smirk until she had her back to Thora.

Startled by her owner's sudden movements, Thora canted her head and watched Halcyon vanish beyond the stable's entrance. Just as she reached for the pitchfork, Thora thought she heard a low laugh, but she brushed it off. Continuing with her punishment, she needed to finish so she could prepare the next meal for Halcyon but only after a quick bath. The gods knew she needed one.

* * *

Later that afternoon, Thora returned to the quiet home. She had a quick, cold bath and then went directly to the supply room. It was obvious that Cesare had gone to the agora for food and drawn the daily water. She silently thanked him.

Thora gathered the items she needed and went to the kitchen. She quickly prepared a meal for Halcyon, who expected it within an hour. Right on the mark, Cesare barged into the kitchen.

"Finished?" He pointed at the tray full of food.

"*Já.*"

Cesare went over to the wine oinochoe. He pointed at the food and said, "*Andron*."

Thora was confused by the order, although she clearly understood it. "No me," she attempted in ruined Greek tongue.

Cesare shook his head and pointed at Thora. "Yes." He pointed at the kitchen door. "Go." He sighed at Thora's hesitation, so he offered a smile. "It is okay."

From the first day in Greece, Thora was told that women were forbidden to enter the andron, a social room only for men. On occasions, female slaves could go to the andron, but that was only with the master's permission. However, Thora had not met the master of the house. Still, Thora was hardly in the mood to clean the stables again so soon. She put aside her concerns and crossed the courtyard into the andron. She paused in the doorway and settled her gaze on Halcyon, who was seated in an ornate chair.

Halcyon wore a soft purple chiton, sandals, and a necklace. She appeared much less threatening in her daily attire than her hoplite uniform. She signaled for Thora to come to her.

Once in the room, Thora noted the young man seated on a kline to the left of Halcyon. She averted her eyes to

Halcyon, who indicated the cleared table on her right. Thora set the tray of food down and stepped to the side.

Halcyon noted Thora's keen interest in the newcomer, Yarikh.

Yarikh met the unusual slave's curious stare. His brown eyes twinkled, and a slight grin pulled at his lips. He was young, but his thin beard added the appearance of age.

"Thora?" Halcyon frowned when Thora ignored her. She leaned forward and snared Thora's wrist. Thora instinctively jumped away from Halcyon.

"*It okay,*" Yarikh said in Thora's native tongue.

Thora went still, and her attention jerked to the stranger, who spoke familiar words from her homelands. "*You know my language?*"

Halcyon released Thora and listened to Yarikh's foreign conversation.

"*I know... a tiny.*"

Thora's lips tugged with a smile. His tongue was hardly perfect. She opened her mouth to say more but was cut off by Halcyon's thick voice.

"Stop."

Thora's words shattered, and she glanced at Halcyon. She inwardly sighed, yet her curiosity was leveled on the newcomer.

"I am already impressed, Yarikh."

Yarikh bowed his head, then smiled at his prospective client. "I spent many years with a merchant. He had a keen interest in the lands to the north. I picked up some of their words for trade."

"Did you travel to those lands?" Halcyon asked.

Yarikh nodded. "We traveled into parts of Germania but not farther. They are dangerous lands, dangerous people."

Halcyon considered Thora, who was strong-willed and probably embodied her northern homelands. She pointed at her tray of food. "Would you like anything?"

"I am fine, but thank you." Yarikh folded his hands in his lap. "Has she learned any Greek?"

"Only simple words." Halcyon paused. "She is good at deciphering body language and tones."

"I imagine so." Yarikh lifted his attention to the silent slave.

As Halcyon reached for the grape bowl, she asked, "Have you seen Germanics similar to her in your travels?"

Yarikh studied Thora, who had golden hair and milky skin. He had seen granite blue eyes in Germania, but Thora's were much brighter. "Similar," he said finally.

Halcyon took a drink of wine. "What is different?"

"Germanics do not have hair as light as hers. Her skin is also rather pale for a Germanic." Yarikh tilted his head. "You say her name is Thora?"

Halcyon gave a nod.

Yarikh bit his lower lip for a beat. "I have not heard the name before." He looked at Halcyon. "Would you like me to question her about where she is from while you eat?"

Halcyon was curious about Thora's background. She had been waiting three months to find out. "Yes."

Yarikh smiled because he knew Halcyon was as curious as he about Thora's history. "Yð nafn ist Thora?"

Thora considered the stranger's odd dialect. She had heard it after she was taken from her homelands. She was able to piece together his question. "*Já.*"

"*I, Yarikh.*"

Thora nodded and was certain the name was Greek or Roman.

"*Can explain where are from?*" Yarikh asked.

Thora narrowed her eyes at the choppy tongue and shook her head.

Yarikh rubbed his beard and said, "*Your home.*"

Thora understood the most important word. "*Home is far north of here.*"

Yarikh grasped fragments of Thora's reply. The language he had learned in his travels was a dialect of Thora's native tongue. But it was enough to break the barrier. "*Are you from Germania?*"

Thora had heard the name Germania for the people south of her homelands. She shook her head and replied, "*Much farther north.*" She raised her left fist level to her chest. "*Germania.*" She then lifted her right hand above her head. "*Norsk.*"

"*Norsk?*" Yarikh repeated, having yet to hear of such lands.

Listening to the fragmented conversation, Halcyon studied Thora's attempt to show Yarikh her homelands. "Is that not Scandia?"

Yarikh looked at Halcyon, who was obviously well educated. "Scandia is farther north than Germania." He gazed upon the unusual slave. "I have not journeyed there."

Thora looked from Yarikh to Halcyon. "Norsk." She frowned at the name they called her homelands. "No... Scandia."

Halcyon popped a grape in her mouth. Her grin appeared due to Thora's proud correction. "I imagine... Norsk are cold lands." She grinned wider at Yarikh. "She carries a fire within her that keeps her warm."

Chuckling, Yarikh imagined it was true. The times he interacted with Germanic slaves, he was impressed by their determination. People from the north were forged from iron.

Halcyon set down the bowl of grapes and focused on her guest. "I am pleased, Yarikh." She crossed her legs and placed her hands in her lap. "Can you teach her Greek?" She wished to communicate with Thora. Halcyon also knew Thora would remain a barbarian in Sparta if she failed to master Greek.

Yarikh had a natural gift for foreign language, diverse in Greek, Latin, and Phoenician. He knew pieces of Germanium dialect, but he was hardly fluent in it. However, it was a challenge rather than a hindrance. "Yes, I believe so."

Halcyon nodded. She was pleased her contact in Athens was able to produce a capable tutor for Thora. "And what of your other employer?"

"I completed my duties with Tyre after we arrived in Athens." Yarikh recalled receiving Halcyon's message, which was perfect timing. He would have returned to Tyre and sought another position with a new merchant, but he was tired of the travel and welcomed the break in Sparta.

"I am at your service," Yarikh said. He bowed his head.

"I will have my slave, Cesare, bring your things into the house. You will have your own quarters here." Halcyon sipped on more wine, then asked, "How much coin do you require per month for your services?"

Yarikh calculated the amount of time he would spend with Thora each day. "Fifteen drachmas."

Halcyon thought about his offer. In Athens, a common household brought home a *triobol* per day. An average Athenian hoplite's wage was one drachma. Yarikh was hardly a hoplite, yet he was skilled as a translator. "Twenty drachmas a month."

Smiling, Yarikh's eyes glowed warmly in appreciation, and he readily agreed to Halcyon's wonderful proposition of room, board, food, and twenty drachmas a month. He thanked the gods for his great fortune.

Halcyon was content with the arrangement. Her attention cut to Thora who had been quiet. Halcyon expected to communicate with her within the next few months, now that Yarikh would tutor Thora each day.

Holding Halcyon's eyes, she knew they had made an arrangement, but she was unsure how it affected her. She hoped that Yarikh was here to teach her Greek. The idea seemed outlandish because slave owners strictly viewed their slaves as property. However, Thora believed there was something different about Halcyon from most slave owners. From the first day, Thora was drawn to Halcyon, and she strangely trusted her. Only the Fates truly knew Thora's future.

⟨HAϽTΣR THRΣΣ

Thora stood over a three-legged, stone basin located in the far corner of the kitchen. She had spent much of her late morning simply grinding wheat with a stone but paused when a new presence entered the kitchen.

Halcyon rested her hands on her hips. She glanced at the grain being milled and decided it was ground correctly. To her right stood Yarikh, and behind her was a girl whom Halcyon turned to and said, "Come."

Once the girl stepped around Halcyon, Thora's eyes lit up upon seeing the friendly face. "Glauce." She remembered the girl from Telamon's household.

Halcyon suspected that Thora was familiar with Glauce. "Yarikh, explain to Thora that she will train this new slave."

Yarikh nodded and did his best to explain it to Thora.

After an exchange, Thora understood that Glauce was her responsibility. She was unsure if Glauce's purchase was a sign of her weakness in the house. "*Is Glauce replacing me*?" she asked in her native tongue.

Yarikh failed to translate the question but attempted answering in Thora's language. "*Show Greek you.*"

Thora opened her mouth to ask more, but she faltered. Her question was too complex for Yarikh's meager skills in a strange dialect. She read Halcyon's features and concluded that Halcyon showed no signs of displeasure with her. Glauce's purchase was not a threat to her place in the household.

Glauce remained quiet with her head down. Her short, brown curls curtained around her face. She continued being as small as possible even if she was relieved that it was Thora.

"*Glauce — kitchen.*" Thora pointed at the girl slave and then at the kitchen. She nodded, firmly.

"*Þak,*" Yarikh said. He hoped he had properly thanked Thora.

Thora shook her head at Yarikh's error and corrected him. "*Þakka fyrir.*"

Yarikh smiled at Thora teaching him. He made a mental note to trade teachings. "*Þakka fyrir.*"

Thora mirrored the smile. "*Ekki at þakka.*"

Yarikh suspected it was the polite response to the thanks. He then noticed Halcyon had carefully watched their exchange. He straightened his back.

Halcyon was pleased that Thora understood her plans. She was about to leave but said, "Selene... tonight." She chose to ignore the annoyed spark on Thora's face.

Yarikh waited until Halcyon was gone, then he said, "Greek at first light."

"*Já.*" Thora was excited to learn Greek tomorrow. She bid goodbye to Yarikh, then touched Glauce's shoulder and smiled at the girl, guessing that Glauce was four or so years younger. "You cook."

Giving a shy nod, Glauce shadowed her teacher in the kitchen for the day. Together, they made fresh bread for the upcoming three days. Next, they began preparing the evening meal for everyone, which included Selene. Thora attempted controlling her frustration that Linnr was in the house tonight. It had only been two nights ago that she had spilled wine on Selene.

Later, Cesare arrived in the kitchen and announced that Selene was in the courtyard with Halcyon. There were at least three hours until sunset. A nice meal in the courtyard was common for Greeks. Cesare assisted Glauce with taking the first dishes to the courtyard. Thora noticed that Glauce had forgotten the wine, so she hastened out of the kitchen with the filled oinochoe.

In the courtyard, Halcyon sat beside Selene on a bench. In front of them was a table. Halcyon took a handful of grapes and nearly asked for wine until Thora approached them.

"Go to Selene," Halcyon said to Glauce.

She bowed her head after Thora came in with the the wine. Glauce was abashed that she had forgotten it, but Thora gave her a compassionate look. Glauce offered the board of finger foods to Selene.

Thora picked up the empty skyphos from the iron table in front of the freewomen. She poured it carefully then held it out to Halcyon.

"*Þakka fyrir*," Halcyon said softly.

Pausing, Thora wondered if she had truly heard Halcyon's appreciation in the Norsk tongue. Halcyon's next command cut through her awe.

"Serve Linnr." Halcyon was stern, but a glint showed in her eyes.

Thora bit her smirk. "*Já*, ěra."

Selene must have caught wind of the conversation and asked, "Liner?"

Halcyon shook her head. "Linnr."

Thora was pouring wine in the remaining empty skyphos, then offered it to Selene.

"What is Linnr?"

Halcyon shrugged, but amusement laced her tone. "That is your name in her native tongue." Thora's drawing in the dirt from earlier today came back to her. After her broken conversation with Thora, she recognized the snakelike traits about Selene that she had ignored. Her heart was heavy with the truth.

"Oh." Selene accepted the skyphos from Thora. "It sounds different than Selene."

"Well, you know that barbaric tongue," Halcyon said mockingly.

Thora backed away from Selene, who sat next to Halcyon on a bench. She decided that they both were comfortable and that Glauce or Cesare could care for them. She left for the kitchen but paused on hearing Linnr's voice.

"Why do you waste your time, Halcyon?"

"A good wife can communicate with her slaves."

"Next time, select one that speaks Greek."

Thora rolled her eyes and muttered, "Linnr." She slipped into the kitchen and began preparing the main dish.

Selene indicated Glauce. "She speaks Greek."

Halcyon considered Selene's argument. "A slave that is forgetful is not an efficient slave."

Glauce flinched and hoped she had a swift punishment later.

"It just seems such a waste of time and coin," Selene said.

"You are still bitter about the wine, Selene."

Selene bit her tongue, stopping her brooding further about Thora spilling the wine on her finest chiton.

Halcyon decided on a change of topic. "Has your father selected a husband?"

Selene instantly smiled. "I am preparing for pretrial marriage."

"I see your hair has not been cut," Halcyon said. "So I must have a few nights left with you."

"A couple of months. My father is preparing the dowry."

Halcyon grinned at the news. "Does he follow my father's example?"

Selene laughed and shook her head. "No father has followed yours in a while, because you have not given your husband these lands."

"And why should I?" Halcyon had inherited her father's fortunes from his days in Athens. "My husband is not the master of my house." She held out her hands toward the villa around them. "I am the husband of my home." She lowered her hands to her lap.

For a moment, Halcyon drifted back to her days with her father, who had passed into Elysium seven years ago. Her father was from Athens and made his mark in trading with the Phoenicians. Later he met Halcyon's Spartan mother, who wooed him into trading weapons with the Spartans. For several years, her parents lived in Athens and continued amassing fortunes through trade. But Halcyon's mother fell ill only a few years after Halcyon's birth, and they soon moved to Sparta. The sole purpose behind the move was for Halcyon. Sparta's advanced social standards for women were known throughout Greece, and Halcyon's father wanted to ensure his only child inherited his hard work. Such thoughts about the past broke and fractured under Selene's voice.

"Yes, as many other wives, but they have all signed over their lands to their husbands. That is the agreement of the marriage."

Halcyon shook her head. "Over two-thirds of the women in Sparta own the lands. And why?" She crossed her legs under her chiton. "It is because our husbands are busy in the barracks."

Selene inhaled then slowly released it. "They must father our sons." She held her tongue, not wishing to greatly anger Halcyon. Much of her sexual attraction to Halcyon was because Halcyon was the man of her house. What excited her even greater was that Halcyon was a royal guard to the king. In Selene's most construed fantasies, she saw Halcyon as her husband. "Fortunately, Euclid has never seen it fit to loan you to another."

Halcyon grunted and took a long drink of her wine. She leaned forward and placed the empty skyphos on the table. "Euclid wishes I become pregnant, so he can have a son." It was customary for a thirty-five-year-old Spartan woman to have three or more children with another on the way.

"Why have you not?" Selene asked.

"Pregnancy eludes me," Halcyon replied. She loathed explaining how her sexual relations were timed with Euclid. She rarely had a cycle anymore, which was often the sign of an unhealthy woman. In her younger days, they had been regular each month, but her cycles decreased after she joined the hoplite army.

"You must time it more properly." Selene frowned. "Soon you will lose all chance to bear a son for Sparta."

"I let the Fates decide." Halcyon's tone held note that she wished to conclude the discussion.

Selene had agitated her lover, and misunderstood why, but kept quiet.

Shortly, Thora emerged with the first plate of food. She signaled Glauce to retrieve the others. Cesare refilled the skyphoi then left for the evening. He had to attend to his other chores in the stable before dark.

After the meal, Halcyon left to relieve herself. Selene signaled for Glauce to refill her wine. She set the filled skyphos on the table and imagined her pending night in bed with Halcyon. She always looked forward to Halcyon's dominating disposition. Selene's daydream broke when Thora approached the table.

Thora held a sweet bread for the freewoman and noticed her owner was gone.

Selene narrowed her eyes at Thora, who ignored her glare and gently placed the dish on the table. Before Thora could straighten up, Selene snared her wrist. Selene was on her feet already and jerked Thora forward, nearly making her fall on the table.

Thora balanced herself and yanked her wrist free. She straightened with power and pride. Selene seethed at the confidence in Thora. "You owe me for your insult from last time, barbar."

"*Go to Hell, serpent,*" Thora said hotly in her native tongue.

Selene tasted the venom in the reply. A hot red blur passed Selene's vision, and she struck Thora across the cheek. Thora gritted her teeth and touched her burning cheek. She fisted her hands in a fierce attempt to restrain herself.

"You Cerberus!" Selene sneered and continued her rant. "You are jealous of me. But you will never be anything, you worthless horse shit!" She raised her hand, needing to hit again.

Thora silently willed the freewoman to try again. Selene's attempt to belittle her failed each time.

Selene's hand came to an abrupt stop just a breath from Thora's cheek. A strong hand wrapped painfully around her wrist and started squeezing even harder. Selene gaped at Halcyon, who loomed angrily over her.

Thora smirked at Linnr's shocked expression. She was relieved when she first saw Halcyon return behind Selene.

"Never touch my slaves, Selene," Halcyon growled. She yanked Selene against her body with her wrist. "Thora already paid her debt for what she did that night."

"To you — not to me." Selene pulled on her trapped wrist, but Halcyon's grip was iron. "You are too easy on her, Halcyon."

"This is my home." Halcyon lowered her head closer to Selene's own. "And you are not fit for it right now." She threw Selene's wrist from her grasp. "Leave."

Selene swallowed nervously at Halcyon's enraged expression. She gathered her wits and walked around her lover but glared at Halcyon standing defensively in front of her slave. "I hear what they call you, Halcyon. They call you an Amazon. You are unnatural like the Amazons." Her eyes narrowed, and her tone gained acid. "How fitting that you should have such a barbaric slave!"

Halcyon grew quite smug. "If I recall correctly, it is this body-" She signaled her own. "-that you often fantasize about. A pity you will not find a husband or a maiden that will match me." She nonchalantly waved off Selene and turned her back on her former lover.

Selene trembled and stormed out of the courtyard. She left the iron gate open, in final protest to Halcyon and her barbarian.

Halcyon faced Thora. She carefully touched Thora's cheek, which had healed from last time.

Thora gathered Halcyon's hand into her own. "Okay now."

Halcyon smiled sadly at Thora's attempt to speak to her. "Selene is a linnr." Her words caused Thora to grin, and she squeezed the larger hand that was inside of hers.

"Thank you."

Halcyon frowned at the unnecessary praise for intervening with Selene. She had been protecting her property. Yet, Halcyon realized it was far more than just damaged property. Halcyon only moved with such speed and rage during combat, in the name of Sparta. Selene's attack on Thora was hardly against Sparta.

Halcyon could only imagine what rumors Selene would spread about her and Thora. She had to ignore it because her position in the polis and army were higher than most rumors. Soon, Selene would become just another maiden in Halcyon's sexual history.

CHAPTER FOUR

"**O**kay?" Thora asked after she set down a sack of grain on a table in the supply room. She and Glauce had recently returned from the agora.

Glauce shoved her sack that contained a mix of meats, vegetables, and fruits. "Yes." She smiled, enjoying their developing conversations as Thora learned more from her tutor.

Gradually, Thora's duties were reduced so that she could learn Greek. She often handled making meals as per Halcyon's request. Halcyon enjoyed Thora's cooking style, which was mostly Greek with a flair of Norsk.

Thora patted the girl's shoulder, then decided to find Yarikh. He typically would wait for her out in the courtyard where it was empty and quiet. Beyond the villa, an occasional yell followed by a low thud came from the yard. Thora followed the noise behind the house and past the stable. She came to a grass clearing between the stable and the fields where the helots worked the summer crop. Briefly, Thora thanked her gods she was a house slave rather than one belonging to the polis. Her thoughts were cut short by taps and thuds.

Halcyon wore a simple, white tunic and a short skirt. She hefted a long *dory* closer to the spiked end while the spear tip faced forward. With a honed skill, she repeatedly attacked the large wood post with the dory's spearhead.

Staring in amazement, Thora stood to one side while Halcyon practiced several types of thrusts with the dory. She understood why Halcyon was so incredibly muscular. Thora could hardly imagine the strength and endurance it took to constantly drive such a long weapon at an enemy.

Cesare was near Halcyon and stood at attention. To the right of his foot were two damaged dory spears. The heads had been snapped off from Halcyon's practices.

Yarikh stood behind and slightly off to the side, observing Halcyon's intense hoplite training, which he had often heard about in Rome. Thora silently came up and stood beside her tutor.

Halcyon sensed her slave's presence but remained focused on her training. After numerous attacks, she finally snapped the spearhead. Halcyon spun the dory and used the counterbalance spiked end for a weapon. She drove it into the wood and slashed her wooden opponent.

Thora was impressed by Halcyon's prowess as a hoplite. "Fallegur," she whispered to herself. Then a sudden blush dusted her cheeks. She was fortunate nobody could translate her compliment about Halcyon's physique.

Yarikh glanced at Thora, but he was unsure of the word. He suspected it was a compliment from the way Thora was admiring Halcyon.

Completing the drill, Halcyon tossed the broken dory by the other two and approached Cesare, who gave her the sheathed xiphos. Halcyon accepted it, then went over to Yarikh and Thora. "Are you going to practice today?"

Yarikh nodded. "We will be in the courtyard."

Halcyon cool features were broken by a thin smile. "Is Thora learning quickly?"

"She is efficient." Yarikh smiled at Thora but explained to Halcyon the slight difficulties. "The languages can be quite different, especially certain sounds."

Halcyon agreed after she had learned a handful of words from Yarikh.

Yarikh turned to Thora and softly said, "Let us start."

Thora left with her tutor. One time she glanced over her shoulder at Halcyon, who practiced with the short blade. Hopefully, soon she would be allowed to ask Halcyon more about her life as a warrior.

* * *

From sun high to sunset, Yarikh and Thora sat in the courtyard on the warm day and practiced Thora's Greek. Yarikh was pleased by Thora's interests in the language. He suspected it helped that Thora was less drained from her daily chores. She often grew frustrated if she was tired. Halcyon's decision to purchase another slave for some of Thora's duties had been an excellent decision.

When there was an hour of sunlight left, the lessons came to an end. Thora was mentally exhausted, yet she wanted to help Glauce with the evening meal. Normally, Halcyon would have been served by now, but Glauce was probably behind or Halcyon requested it to be later.

From the courtyard entrance, Thora went into the kitchen. She found Glauce stirring the contents of a pot over an open fire. At the central table, Thora took stock of what was tonight's dinner. The items were simple and easy, but Thora was unsure what Glauce had in the pot over the fire.

Glauce still had her back to Thora and was unaware of her arrival. She continued stirring the contents and held a filled oinochoe. Eventually, she began pouring the oinochoe's contents into the pot until Thora's movements scared her.

Thora was just as startled by Glauce's squeal. She then yelled at Glauce when the liquid from the oinochoe spilled into the fire.

Glauce screamed at her mistake, but it was too late. The fire flared and hungrily burned her hand. Glauce dropped the oinochoe into the fire and stumbled back.

The oinochoe smashed into the burning logs and shattered all over the fire. The fatty liquid fed the fire, which dangerously roared like Cerberus. The flames jumped onto Glauce's chiton and attacked her chest and face.

"Glauce!" In two wide steps, Thora jumped, knocked Glauce to the ground, and smothered the flames on her chiton. She scrambled to her feet when the thick smoke filled her lungs. "Up!"

Glauce was hauled to her feet and shoved from the fireplace. With watery eyes, she stared in awe at the thick, gray smoke that twisted up from the fire and billowed across the white ceiling. Her attention snapped to the left when Cesare barged in from the outside door.

Cesare had seen the smoke pipe out from the kitchen's single window during his walk from the stable. He stared wide-eyed at Thora's attempt to get near the fire. He looked to Glauce and ordered, "Go tell ěra!"

Glauce raced out to the courtyard.

"Thora, here!" Cesare indicated the washtub full of water.

Thora coughed several times but hurried over to Cesare. Together, they hefted the basin from its stand and carried it to the uncontrollable fire. With synchronized strength, they poured the water over the fireplace.

Blinking against the irritating smoke, Cesare expected the fire to be extinguished, but instead, it stretched out to the walls and the ceiling with eagerness. Like Thora, he dropped the washtub and tumbled back from the sharp heat that cut his exposed skin. He hit the stone floor, head first. His blurry vision darkened despite the fire's brightness.

"Cesare?" Thora was forced to dance between the flames that had washed over the floor from the water. She touched his face and damp shoulders, but he was unconscious. "*Dritt*," she cursed in her native tongue.

Only Cesare's soft moan gave Thora the strength to act fast. It would take too long to get to the entrance that went into the house. Instead, she got to her feet with Cesare in her arms. She carried him through the back door and was overwhelmed by the fresh air. After setting him down, she reentered the kitchen in hopes to stop the fire.

The blaze had become a mindless creature that quickly spread down the adjacent wall, which held countless wooden shelves for all the cookware. Similarly, the ceiling was consumed by hot red tendrils, and the wood beams glowed brighter than ever. But it was the dense smoke that filled Thora's lungs.

Every one of Thora's thoughts slowed as her mind clouded and sweat coated her skin. She wanted to save the kitchen for Halcyon, but it was hopeless. As she turned to leave, an overhead cracking sound made her peer up. Her yell broke free when the falling timber blocked the back door to the outside, forcing Thora into the center of the kitchen and closer to the raging source. She was coughing and teary-eyed from the smoke, so she lowered herself to the floor for fresh air. The courtyard entrance was only steps away, but now it felt like a walk through Hel.

Urging her weakened body, Thora crawled across the damp floor but slumped when her deprived lungs tightened and made her light-headed. Her slow thoughts turned into weak prayers to her gods. Then, distantly, she heard her gods call her name, again and again.

"Thora!"

Halcyon rushed through the courtyard entrance, and the smoke attacked her. "Thora!" Her heart pounded more each time Thora did not respond to her. She was forced to hunch down. The only help was the smoke escaping into the courtyard or through the single window.

As if traversing Hades itself, Halcyon feverishly sought out her slave. Under the fire's light, she made out the golden hair in all the smoke.

"Thora?" Halcyon coughed and shook her head as she reached Thora's side. She prayed that her slave was more than a dead body. She inhaled deeply, slipped her arms under Thora, and stood up with her. She thanked the gods for her training and strength as a hoplite.

A deafening snap overhead made Halcyon's heart skip a beat. She heard the central timber coming down on them. She gave a battle cry and raced forward, toward the exit to the courtyard. The burning timber nearly swiped her back, but she made it through the doorway and collapsed in the courtyard.

Thora gave a low moan when her body collided with the floor. She rolled out of Halcyon's strong arms.

While coughing hard, Halcyon waited for her watery vision to return to normal. Behind her, the smoke billowed out of the kitchen. She reached for Thora and continued moving her. Halcyon needed to clear the villa, so she staggered to her feet. After a deep breath, she hooked her arms under Thora's own. Thora was limp in Halcyon's arms.

She was tall but mostly lean, which made it easier for Halcyon to drag her away from the kitchen.

Yarikh was beyond the gate at the front of the house. He rushed to Halcyon, who settled Thora on the stone street. "Are you... is Thora?"

Halcyon swallowed and worriedly said, "She is breathing." She was relieved by the arrival of many neighbors. They formed a bucket brigade that stretched from the well in the courtyard to the kitchen's door. Halcyon was grateful for her neighbors' dedication to snuff out the fire.

Shortly, a healer, Giles, arrived and checked each person. Halcyon had him start with Thora, who remained unconscious. He only noted a minor burn on her right arm that would heal in time. Next, Giles took care of Cesare and decided he had worse burns on his left arm, ankles, and face. He also noted a knot at the back of Cesare's head that was an indication he fell at some point. Last, Giles looked over Glauce's minor burns, concluding the slaves would need a generous amount of salve for the next few days.

Giles finally approached the owner of the house.

"I am fine," Halcyon said.

Giles frowned and tried again.

"I am fine." Halcyon's tone held no room for argument and she turned to Yarikh. "Do you need the healer?"

Yarikh shook his head.

After a sigh, Giles gave his report to Halcyon, even warning her that Cesare and Thora may be unconscious for days. He also promised Halcyon he would bring the salve soon. Halcyon insisted that the healer return tomorrow for further checks, which he agreed with her.

Halcyon grasped the healer's shoulder. "Thank you for your service."

"Of course, Halcyon." Giles took his leave.

Halcyon approached Yarikh, who was knelt beside the unconscious slaves. "See to them."

"I will." Yarikh received an appreciative pat on his shoulder, then he watched Halcyon hurry off. His eyes lifted to the house's roof, and he noticed the smoke at the right rear from the kitchen. Moments ago, there had been flames. He was amazed how the fire was already being contained by the brigade.

"You are a very fortunate slave," Yarikh said and brushed her hair away.

Halcyon returned after speaking with the leader of the brigade. They waited for clearance to return home. So far, it appeared that only the kitchen was lost. She considered what had happened in the kitchen, thinking was strange for Thora to be sloppy.

After a sigh, Halcyon turned back to the open gate and listened to the distant yells from the brigade. She studied Glauce, who was the only slave conscious after the fire. Glauce was nervous, and Halcyon suspected the reason. She would find out more once Cesare and Thora were well again.

CHAPTER FIVE

A very low moan escaped from Thora's dry lips. She coughed and tried opening her aching eyes. Her body hurt although her surroundings were comfortable. The air was fresh from the open window, but the smell of medicine wafted under her nose.

"Thora?"

The familiar voice pushed Thora to blink a few times. She smiled at Yarikh and his concerned face. "*Ek feigr?*"

Yarikh translated one word, which was "death." He chuckled and shook his head. "*Nei.*"

Thora was clearly relieved to be alive and listened to Yarikh's steps fade away. After a moment, she realized the room was not her and Glauce's usual one, and it was normally reserved for a guest. The bed was incredibly comfortable compared to her normal sleeping roll on the floor. She attempted moving but was too sore. From the open window,

Thora could see it was late afternoon, but she was unsure about the day.

Shortly, Halcyon appeared in the bedroom and took the wooden chair by the bed. Thora attempted sitting upright until a firm hand made her lie down again.

"*Nei.*" Halcyon crossed her legs. "How do you feel?"

Thora considered the Greek words she could use to reply. "Tired... hurt."

"I know." Halcyon hoped it would improve soon.

"How long?" Thora asked. Her rough accent cut into each word.

"Nearly two days." Halcyon saw the displeasure in Thora's eyes, but movement at the door caught her eye. She allowed Glauce to serve bread, wine, and cheese to Thora.

"Cesare?"

Halcyon nodded. "Cesare is okay."

Glauce stood at the foot of the bed. She kept her head down and waited until Thora was finished eating or Halcyon gave her instructions. Halcyon noticed that Glauce avoided eye contact with Thora. She ignored it and removed the skyphos from the tray.

"Glauce?" Thora asked.

Glauce flinched.

Halcyon sensed that Thora was disturbed by Glauce's refusal to acknowledge her. Halcyon curtly said, "Leave us."

Glauce turned on her sandals and departed the room. Thora stared blankly in Glauce's direction. She shook her head and lifted her distraught features to Halcyon. "Why?" She pointed at the door as if it was Glauce.

Halcyon exhaled and replied, "Glauce is upset."

"Up... set?" Thora asked and shook her head.

Halcyon tried another approach. "She is not happy."

"Why?" Thora was confused. "Everybody okay." She ran her fingers through her golden hair.

Halcyon made no comment, held out a bowl of cheese, and said, "Eat."

Thora sat up and accepted the bowl, but she was deep in thought while she ate. It appeared that Halcyon's home and slave had been spared from the fire.

Halcyon had pieced together what most likely happened the other evening. However, she had yet to find out the facts and waited for Cesare and Thora.

After the fire, Giles periodically visited and checked on the injured slaves. Thora had awoken briefly but had fallen back to sleep until now. Cesare gained consciousness shortly after Thora had awoken the first time. Giles instructed that Cesare stay bedridden until his memory returned completely.

He was less concerned about Thora, who was recovering much faster. Giles continuously applied a salve to the slaves' burns.

At night, Halcyon slipped into the room and discovered a sense of peace from Thora's deep, constant breaths. Halcyon had spent many hours with Thora and tried sorting out her thoughts about the fire. Tonight would probably be the same.

* * *

By the next day, Thora was out of bed and moving through the villa. Her chores had been greatly reduced and given to Glauce. Several times she attempted to help, until caught by Halcyon.

Thora spent her time visiting Cesare, who was still healing. They hardly spoke, but she was glad to see his beautiful brown eyes, his smile, and his salt and pepper hair. Since the fire, he had slipped into her heart. She missed her family deeply, but Cesare was becoming a father figure to her.

On the third day after Thora woke up, Yarikh resumed their lessons. Soon, Thora was back to cooking evening meals for Halcyon, at least as best as possible. A temporary kitchen had been set up in the supply room. Then one afternoon, Halcyon ordered Thora, Cesare, and Yarikh into the andron. Halcyon sat at the head kline, legs crossed, and her features stern. She had the slaves stand while Yarikh sat on the left kline.

"Cesare, you were in the kitchen with Glauce?"

Cesare nodded. "Not at first, ĕra. I was finishing up at the stable. As I neared the back door to the kitchen, I saw smoke coming from the window and rushed in. Glauce and Thora were fighting the fire."

Thora listened even though she only caught fragments.

"I told Glauce to find you," Cesare said.

Halcyon pictured the story Cesare painted for her.

"Then Thora and I tried to throw the water from the washtub onto the fire. It seemed to make it worse, because the fire exploded. I fell, hit my head, and went unconscious."

Halcyon nodded, then her eyes flickered over to Thora. "What can you tell me, Thora?"

Breaking from the memories, Thora mentally composed her thoughts into Greek words. "I finish lesson with Yarikh. I went help Glauce with cooking." Thora drifted back to the dangerous night. "Glauce not know I there and scared her. She dropped a oinochoe into the fire."

Halcyon realized that the oinochoe had contained the fat that fed the fire. She gave a soft nod for Thora to continue her account.

"Glauce burning. I jump her to ground." Thora paused and sighed at her choppy Greek, thankful that Halcyon was patient. "Cesare come... help with water." She glanced at him. "I got out Cesare and went back kitchen." She frowned at her memories and how eerie it had been to lose her thoughts, her strength, and finally her consciousness. "I not breathe. I try stop fire, but I had nothing." Her distraught expression lowered from meeting Halcyon's gaze. "I crawl like child over floor." She combed her fingers through her hair. "No hope." She shook her head. "I... fell asleep."

"You fell unconscious," Yarikh said.

"Unconscious," Thora repeated, the word now locked in her vocabulary. Her curious features rested on Halcyon. "Why do I live?"

Halcyon lowered her hands to her lap. "I carried you out."

Thora shook her head because she misunderstood a few of the words.

Cesare saw Thora's confusion but pointed at their owner and then stepped closer to Thora, pretending to pick her up. "Carry you."

Thora gratefully looked at Halcyon and sincerely said, "Thank you."

Halcyon dipped her head in acknowledgement.

Thora asked, "I work now?"

Halcyon weighed the request, now that the two slaves were well again. She placed her hands behind her back, on the kline. "You may start tomorrow."

Thora was relieved. She was enjoying her lessons with Yarikh but was also ready to continue her duties. "The kitchen?"

Halcyon arched an eyebrow at how talkative Thora had become now that Yarikh was teaching her Greek. She was pleased and realized it would change their dynamics. "It will be rebuilt."

Thora glanced at her teacher. "Rebuilt?"

"Another kitchen," Yarikh replied.

Thora nodded.

Halcyon then excused the three and thought about the kitchen fire. It appeared it was solely Glauce's actions that destroyed the kitchen, risking the other two slaves. Halcyon's anger from that night resurfaced and boiled under her skin.

* * *

The next morning, Thora started her normal routine, including grinding the grain for the evening. She asked Cesare whether Glauce had left to go to the agora to purchase the grain, vegetables, and meats. He replied that Glauce was still drawing water from the well in the courtyard.

Shortly, Glauce emerged in the temporary kitchen in the supply room. She gathered the empty satchel for the trip to the agora.

"Glauce," Cesare said.

Glauce paused and looked at Cesare.

"Ĕra wishes to see you before you go."

Visibly pale, Glauce returned the satchel and silently left.

Thora was confused until Cesare explained that Halcyon required Glauce in the andron. Thora's stomach suddenly pitched with worry and drove her out of the supply room. Cesare's yell went ignored until he snared her wrist. She turned thunderous blue eyes on him.

Cesare sighed at Thora's rebellious nature. He worried more for Thora than Halcyon, but he could do nothing to halt Thora, letting her arm slide free.

Thora walked around the courtyard's pool and approached the andron's sealed doors. Rarely were they ever closed, but she peered through the thin crack.

Glauce nervously stood in the center of the andron. To her left, Halcyon glared darkly at her. She circled Glauce as if she were prey.

"It is because of your foolishness that I have lost my kitchen." She paused, but the venom seeped in her voice. "I must rebuild the kitchen." She stood behind the shaking slave. "You endangered two of my slaves." She continued pacing around Glauce until she was in front of her again. "And I nearly died trying to save Thora."

Glauce closed her eyes, and tears trickled down her cheeks.

"Do not cry, slave," Halcyon said fiercely. "You make a mistake in life, and you must pay a price for it." She walked behind Glauce, then suddenly struck her in the back of the head.

Glauce shrieked as she fell to her knees in a ball. Halcyon's eyes darkened at the pathetic display. She was prepared to punish Glauce further.

"No!" Thora burst into the andron and stood protectively between the scared slave and her furious owner. "Do not punish Glauce." She defiantly towered over her owner. "It is my punishment." There was a brief silence other than Glauce's whimpers.

Halcyon's jaw was clenched and knuckles white. She sneered at Thora's disobedience and raised her fist, yet paused in midair. Thora held her position and silently dared Halcyon.

"I fail. Glauce does not cook. I do. I late, so she tried to help." She pointed at the frail girl behind her. "You cannot punish her for it."

Halcyon was breathing heavier each moment, Thora's speech giving her pause.

"Hit me," Thora said, demandingly, and braced herself.

Halcyon's fury was sliced in half by the surprising command. Every single punishment she gave to Thora did nothing to kill the thunderous nature. Halcyon learnt that certain individuals could never be truly enslaved. If she hit Thora now, it would be purely in anger and not punishment. Gradually, her fist lowered, and her rage washed away.

"Leave, Thora." Halcyon hid the tremble in her hands and was spent by the argument. "Take Glauce with you." After a moment of stillness, she snapped, "Now!"

Thora broke from her bewilderment, turned, and hooked the girl's arms. In soft murmurs, she coaxed Glauce to her feet and hurried them from the andron.

Halcyon heard the door seal shut. For a long moment, she stood motionless and lost by what happened between her and Thora. She prided herself on control, both over herself and her slaves. But it had slipped through her hands today. Halcyon feared it was Thora who held the control this time.

Enraged again, she yelled and snatched the nearest kline by its back. With a need to fight against her fears, she threw the kline across the room. It smashed into another kline, which hit the wall and cracked two of its legs. Silence cut through the andron until Halcyon's sandals slapped against the floor.

Cesare stiffened when Halcyon stormed into the courtyard. He had witnessed bits and pieces of what happened between Halcyon and Thora, but this was the first time he had seen Halcyon lose her self-control.

"Clean the andron by the time I return!" Halcyon vanished out of the gate and went to the stable.

The three remaining horses whinnied when Halcyon stomped into the stable. She went directly to her favored horse, who never went to the games in Olympia. Shoving open the stall door, she felt a brief sense of peace. From childhood, she had loved riding and was gifted a horse by her father. As an adult, Halcyon sent her horses to the games in Olympia and made a small fortune. Today, Halcyon owned a dozen beautiful horses that each had their own special personality.

As Halcyon approached her horse, she gazed into the mare's glossy blue eyes that filled Halcyon with a sense of freedom. The white mare, Cheimon, had been a traditional wedding gift from her husband. In the beginning, she had ignored the gift until she and Cheimon formed a bond after a few rides. She now cherished the rare-colored horse more than the others in the stable.

Cheimon huffed low at her owner. She then shook her head at the human's ugly mood and made no arguments when a bronze bit went into her mouth. But there was no saddle or any other gear. When the human was on her back, the horse slammed her front hoof and excitedly whinnied at Halcyon's needs.

Ducking low, Halcyon urged her horse out of the stable and spurred the horse toward the fields, galloping past the helots working with the crops. The open space and freedom brought relief to Halcyon. She and Cheimon quickly escaped the troubles at home and faded away in the valleys.

CHAPTER SIX

Unlike most hoplites, Halcyon rotated between the barracks and her home. Male hoplites lived full time at the barracks, only venturing home to secure Greece's future. Fortunately, their king arranged that Halcyon and her husband alternated between both. The days until Halcyon would leave for the barracks were long and edgy. She had delayed her return to the barracks after the fire so that she could organize the reconstruction. She had to leave the next day, and her husband, Euclid, would arrive on his break and take over the house duties.

Halcyon had remained quiet during the passing days. Her face was devoid of emotions and her eyes distant. She rarely saw Glauce unless the circumstances were unavoidable.

Otherwise, it seemed as if Thora and Cesare took it upon themselves to protect the girl from their owner.

Halcyon and Thora rarely spoke unless it was to pass commands and orders from owner to slave. Sensing Thora's displeasure, Halcyon tried ignoring it and the way it made her uncomfortable. She was, after all, the slave owner with the control in the house. Regardless, time at the barracks would help ease her own tension and distress. At first light, she would return to the barracks where her brothers-in-arms would greet her. As a hoplite, Halcyon was freed from her bonds as a woman.

* * *

The following morning, Thora rose at dawn and prepared for the day. After she dressed, she went downstairs and noticed Cesare was already performing chores.

"Good morning, Thora."

Thora pleasantly smiled at him. "You up early."

Cesare nodded and said, "I helped Halcyon prepare before dawn."

Thora became confused and asked, "She left?" At Cesare's nod, she frowned. "I did not say farewell."

Cesare neared her. "Halcyon does not require farewells." He then touched her stiff shoulder. "She will be back in a fortnight."

Thora was bothered that Halcyon left with their silence intact. She had barely spoken to her but wanted to settle the dispute but robbed of such a chance.

"Do not worry, Thora." Cesare smiled, then released her shoulder after a soft squeeze. "We must hurry. We have a lot of work to do today."

Thora shook her head then asked, "What work?"

Cesare came closer and said quietly, "*Ěrus* returns tomorrow. Euclid must not know that our ěra goes into the andron."

Thora was confused by the Greek home's segregation compared to her homelands. "Why?"

Cesare gathered his thoughts and sighed at Halcyon's constant need to push the social standards. Perhaps if Halcyon's mother had lived, Halcyon would have grown up differently. "Things will happen in this house that should not if ěrus learns of Halcyon's lifestyle." For years, Cesare took it upon himself to reorganize the villa prior to Euclid's return. "You care for Halcyon?"

"*Já.*"

Cesare smiled at her affirmation. "Then we must hurry." He took Thora's hand and guided her into the andron. They needed to return things to how Euclid would have them and not Halcyon. The klines were arranged differently, the tables set correctly, and a certain favorite sculpture of Ares was always present in the andron. Halcyon favored Athena over Ares, so she often removed the sculpture of Ares once Euclid left home.

Yarikh assisted the slaves with the heavy sculpture. Afterwards, he retired to the courtyard until Thora had time for her lessons. He suspected it would be later in the day. Halcyon had instructed him to watch over Thora in case her newly acquired Greek tongue caused trouble. Yarikh was surprised by the request, but he intended to fulfill it.

As expected, Euclid arrived late the next morning on his horse and in full uniform. His entrance was loud, his gear crashing into the *thalamus* upstairs. He began checking over the latest changes to his home and the future plans for the kitchen. His wife and the local gossip had alerted him about the fire, and while infuriated, he had been assured by Halcyon that the appropriate punishment had been completed by the erring slave. Euclid disbelieved it since Halcyon, like all wives, had a soft spot for slaves.

Finally, Euclid stripped off his tunic and took a much-needed bath.. Cesare took his armor for polishing later. As Euclid sank deep into the bath, the past month and a half in the barracks weighed on him. For over a year, he had been training his young *pais*, and their bond had grown deeper.

A throaty groan escaped Euclid when his memories of training shifted to the previous night's lovemaking between him and his pais, Tycho. Soon, Tycho would be a grown man and was already seeking a wife. He had heard her name, Selene, and she was in her prime for marriage.

It was actually through Tycho that he learned which slave had caused the fire in his house. Selene had informed Tycho that it was the new barbaric slave. Euclid had already laid eyes on the golden-haired slave, and he was impressed by her beauty. Halcyon had incredible taste in picking the female slaves compared to the males.

Euclid went back to imagining his pais, and it aroused him. He reached under the water, and his moans filled the bathing room.

After the bath, Euclid went about his afternoon and took stock of the villa, field, and stables. The following day, Euclid met Yarikh, who was teaching the barbaric slave to speak Greek. He was humored by the sheer idea. It was a waste of Halcyon's coin, but he had little say in the matter.

From the short meeting, Yarikh concluded that Euclid was truly an arrogant Greek. Euclid looked down upon any man who was not Grecian, which included Yarikh. He made sure to instruct Thora to stay away from Euclid, as Yarikh predicted their personalities would erupt. Euclid was hardly forgiving or reasonable, unlike his wife.

Thora did as Yarikh requested but only after he reinforced that it was Halcyon's wish. Thora kept her tongue tied, her head down, and her presence minimal. It was difficult for her, but she respected Yarikh and Halcyon. Thankfully, she rarely dealt with Euclid because Cesare tended to him. Euclid usually spent his time in the andron or the courtyard. Thora and Glauce took care of Halcyon's side of the house. Thora hoped Halcyon's return was soon, especially because it would signal the end of Euclid's stay.

* * *

By the third day, Euclid had men begin reconstruction of the kitchen. He wanted it completed before the autumn equinox. Much of his time was spent helping with the work, as he was quite good with physical labor and construction from his time as a hoplite. By sunset, Euclid was often worn out, and he retired to his room. However, he wanted to host a *symposium* before he left for the barracks that would garner him political popularity among the elders. He forewarned Cesare about the event and ordered the andron to be prepared and certain wines purchased from the agora.

The slaves feverishly worked to prepare for the symposium that would commence in the evening. Thora had to minimize her lessons with Yarikh so she could prepare the food. She required extra time because the temporary kitchen in the supply room was small and ill-equipped.

The night of the political party, Thora found herself as exhausted as Glauce and Cesare, but they pushed through it. Glauce and Thora were permitted to enter the andron under Euclid's instructions so that they could serve his guests. Thora was surprised at how many people arrived at the symposium. Most of the guests were men, and the few women were entertainers of different sorts. Musicians and a bard also arrived to entertain Euclid's happy guests. In the center of the room, two kraters were filled with wine and were quickly being drained by the men.

Thora slipped out of the andron with two large, empty bowls that needed various cheeses. She disappeared into the supply room and hastily retrieved the precut cheese cubes in the linen cloth. Once organized, she hurried out but slowed upon seeing Euclid in the courtyard. Cautiously, Thora went past him and ensured a certain space between them.

Euclid turned in place, then suddenly grabbed Thora's shoulder. "You ignore me, slave."

Thora ground her teeth and held the bowls tighter to keep them from falling out of her hands. She faced him, which broke their physical contact.

Euclid was slightly shorter than Thora, but he was much bulkier and advanced on her. "I was told you set the fire in the kitchen."

Thora detected the wine on his breath that aided his desire to confront her. She kept her eyes off him. Slaves were designed to be submissive, except for Thora. However, she was unsure how long she could play the weak slave for Euclid's benefit.

"Answer me." Euclid yanked her closer.

With strained lines in her brow, Thora's eyes grew stormy and dark despite her pounding heart's warning. She continued holding her silence in hopes Euclid would believe she was weak in the Greek tongue and let her go.

Euclid narrowed his eyes at Thora. "I know you understand me." He tightened his grip on her arm. "Yarikh teaches you day and night. I have heard you speak my tongue." He then growled, "Did you set my kitchen on fire?"

Thora inhaled a deep breath and narrowed her gaze at the master. "Yes, I started fire." She would protect Glauce.

Euclid smirked in triumph. "I knew you understood me." Then her admission drilled deeper into his chest, and he shoved Thora backwards. "You have cost me a lot of coin!" He cut his eyes to the bowl that had shattered on the floor.

Ignoring the broken bowl and scattered cheese, Thora carefully set the other bowl on the bench next to the pool. She fisted her hands, ready to defend herself against the master. Thora hardly viewed him as her owner — only Halcyon.

"You may not have the coin to pay me, but you do have something else."

Thora missed most of his words, yet she read the hunger on his face. With fisted hands, she readied for his attack.

Euclid jumped at Thora, and he took her down to the tiled ground. Barely holding her down, he grunted from the strong punch to his side. "Be still!" He grabbed her throat with one hand and tightened his grip.

Gasping for air, Thora eyes grew wide and she distantly heard a chorus of laughter from the symposium guests. Then her chiton was hiked up, which caused her to battle Euclid again. She swore at him in her native tongue.

Euclid grunted and struggled for dominance over Thora, mildly impressed with her strength. "Be silent."

As dots appeared in her vision, Thora rammed her knee into his side, which gave her a chance to breathe. Euclid lost all patience and raised Thora's upper body by her throat.

He was prepared to slam her back down against the tile until a voice halted him.

"Euclid." Yarikh stood on the other side of the pool. He appeared calm, even in his words. Inwardly, he shook at the sheer thought of Thora's peril. "A dead or pregnant slave is a worthless slave."

Euclid stared hard into Thora's bright blue eyes, seeming to weigh Yarikh's words.

Gasping for air, Thora returned Euclid's stare and truly understood what defined him. He viewed Thora as a lifeless property to be used as it pleased him. There was nothing about Thora that made her of more value, much less another human.

Euclid jerked her throat from his hold and climbed to his feet. He kicked Thora in the side for good measure, then coldly said, "Clean this mess and continue your duties." He went around the pool and met Yarikh.

Yarikh tore his attention from Thora and met Euclid's murderous features.

"You speak to me again, and I will run you through." Euclid left the courtyard and returned to his guests.

Rolling to her side, Thora clenched her teeth and waited for the pain to subside. She released a shaky breath at what nearly happened to her.

Yarikh knelt beside Thora and gingerly touched her shoulder. "Are you okay?"

Closing her eyes, Thora nodded, then attempted standing up, but Yarikh helped her. "Halcyon will be angered." She had defied Euclid, and so had Yarikh.

Yarikh doubted it was true but let it go and asked, "Can you still work?"

"I must," Thora replied. She calmed herself, then knelt until Yarikh grabbed her arm.

"I will find Cesare or Glauce to clean this." Yarikh pointed at the andron. "They need the cheese."

Thora nodded and went to the supply room first, hoping there was another bowl she could use for the cheese.

Yarikh sought out Glauce and asked her to take care of the broken bowl in the courtyard. Glauce hurried off to do so and nearly bumped into Thora. She attempted to ask what had happened, but Thora shook her head and continued to the andron.

Slipping into the andron, Thora placed the two bowls of cheese in their spots and checked that the krater was still full.

Cesare was off to one side, watching the guests and listening to the bard tell stories about the gods. His attention was disrupted when Thora joined his side. Thora stayed close to Cesare, who curiously looked at her. She sensed his rise of concern because of the marks on her neck.

"Thora," Cesare said softly.

"It is fine," Thora brushed it off. She too enjoyed the bard, having heard a few of them in the past, but her improved Greek made it easier to follow the story.

Cesare let out a low but frustrated sigh, silently promising he would find out later what happened to Thora. When he looked over at their master, he suspected what had taken place moments ago. Halcyon would be quite displeased.

CHAPTER SEVEN

Halcyon halted her mare and dismounted beside the familiar stable, her armor clanking when her sandals hit the dirt. Once she had the reins, she guided Cheimon into the stable to a clean stall and enjoyed untacking and brushing her horse.

The brief time alone with Cheimon gave her a chance to reflect on the past two fortnights at the barracks with her comrades. She was always torn between her life as a hoplite and a master of her home. With a heavy sigh, she shifted her mindset to her duties at home and her pending visit with Euclid before he returned to the barracks the next day. Near the end of her care, she smiled at the approaching footfall.

"Cesare."

Bowing his head, Cesare had a smile and warmly offered, "Welcome back, ĕra." He admired Halcyon in her hoplite armor.

"You sound as if you missed me," Halcyon said with good nature.

Cesare chuckled and put his hands behind his back, which made his soft brown chiton sway. "We have been busy. The master is still here and waits for you."

"I am sure," Halcyon said softly. "And busy with what?" She stilled the brush over Cheimon's rump and glanced at Cesare. "I see Euclid began work on the kitchen."

"He did." Cesare paused. "The master had a symposium while you were gone."

Halcyon's lips thinned at the news. "Strange, considering we have no kitchen."

Cesare bit his lower lip then replied, "It did not seem to deter him."

"I see." After setting the brush in the wall rack, Halcyon patted the horse, then pointed at the saddlebags.

Cesare stepped forward and quickly picked up the saddlebags for his owner. He took extra care with the helmet that was tied to the side.

"Did the symposium fair well?" Halcyon asked.

"We managed."

Halcyon nodded, then stepped out of the stall with the rest of the horse tack. She went to the end of the stable and hung up the tack that would be cleaned later. She stood by the doorway. "How does Yarikh fare?"

"He is well, ĕra. He is currently at the agora." Cesare followed her out of the stable. He carried the saddlebags diligently, then took them to the thalamus once in the house.

Halcyon gazed about the courtyard after passing the open gate, finding everything much the same. However, she diverted from the andron since Euclid was home and instead wandered toward the kitchen that was no longer a darkened, ashen mess but nearly new. She was pleased by the progress.

Halcyon's head snapped to the left after something was dropped on the other side of the house. As she crossed the courtyard, she heard low curses in another tongue. She entered the supply room, which had been adjusted for a temporary kitchen. Little to her surprise, Thora was dealing with a broken oinochoe.

"Let us not start another fire, shall we?"

Thora had her back to the supply room's door but whirled around with shards of clay in her hand. Her initial surprise faded from her features as she gazed upon her owner. Thora sadly smiled on seeing the fully armored hoplite before her.

"Welcome home, ĕra."

Halcyon felt uneasy for a beat. "Thank you." She cleared her throat and pointed at the broken oinochoe. "Are there any left?"

Thora glanced at the clay fragments on the floor, holding up a large piece in her hand. "Six or eight now."

Halcyon sighed because her two female slaves, Thora and Glauce, could be clumsy at times. "We will need to make more soon."

"Once kitchen is done." After setting the shards on the table, Thora indicated the bronze armor. "Your training is good?"

"Yes." Halcyon was having a regular conversation with Thora for the first time thanks to Yarikh's teachings. She was more impressed with Thora's Greek tongue than the kitchen's near completeness. "Have you been busy?" Halcyon moved closer to her slave.

"Yes." Thora leaned against the table, her hip on the edge.

"Cesare mentioned my husband had a symposium." Halcyon rested her hand on the xiphos's hilt. She always admired the blue of Thora's eyes and the gold of her hair. Many times, Halcyon looked at the sun in the sky and thought of Thora during her time at the barracks.

"Yes, it went well."

"Did you manage without the kitchen?" Halcyon expected Thora to become confused by her words. However, Thora's Greek tongue was much stronger.

"Yes... it took more time."

Halcyon nodded, and she nearly asked more until the marks on Thora's neck caught her attention. She stepped into Thora's space and removed her hand from the hilt.

Tensing, Thora allowed her owner to touch her tender skin and averted her gaze overtop of Halcyon's head.

"What is this?"

Thora finally looked down into a fiery green stare and replied, "It is nothing."

"Ares's balls," Halcyon said bitterly. "You will tell me who touched you."

Thora stoned her features and wished Halcyon would end the discussion, especially because she had just returned home.

Halcyon was determined to find out the truth, reaching up and pushing the chiton off Thora's shoulders. Once the chiton pooled at her feet, she was able to see the bruising over Thora's now bare side.

Thora clenched her hands and struggled with her nude form in front of Halcyon but had suffered much worse since her enslavement.

"Tell me now why my husband touched you." Halcyon could tell Thora wanted to argue with her, so she quietly said, "Before he tells me."

Thora swallowed her pride. "He fought with me about the fire."

"It was not your fault."

"He believes different." Thora hesitated and bit her bottom lip. "I rather him attack me instead of Glauce."

Narrowing her eyes, Halcyon turned on her heels and returned her hand to the xiphos, almost prepared to draw it. Once out of the courtyard, she called for Cesare, who listened to her instruction.

"I need you to draw a bath for me and have Thora assist you." She started to the steps to go upstairs. "And I want Glauce to prepare the meal."

Thora hastily drew her chiton over her body again. She tightened the straps before Cesare came into the supply room.

Cesare frowned and softly asked, "Did she see?"

"*Já.*"

Cesare blew out a breath but nodded. "Let us hurry." He went in search of Glauce then joined Thora in the bathing room.

Together, they brought buckets of water from the well, warmed them, and filled the in-floor bath. Thora selected Halcyon's favorite oils for the bath. She set them aside, then decided to check on her owner.

Cesare went into the kitchen to see if Glauce needed help. He assisted her with a few things, then left the supply room. He was confused why his owner had yet to come down for her bath. He went upstairs and to the thalamus that Halcyon and Euclid shared on occasion.

"Perfect timing, Cesare," Halcyon said. She instructed Cesare to stand over by Thora.

Cesare remained rooted for a beat and stared uneasily at Halcyon's position under Euclid, who was nude.

Thora had her hands behind her back and nervously glanced at Cesare when he came to her side. She was unsure whether to be grateful for Cesare's company or bothered by the fact they both had to stand witness over the master bedding their owner. Her eyes lowered to her owner's bronze armor, which leaned against the wall. She lifted her attention when Halcyon spoke to Euclid.

"It has been so long."

Euclid was ravaging his wife's neck with his mouth. "Too long, Halcyon."

"You cannot leave tomorrow without first having me," Halcyon whispered in his ear. She raised her bare, muscular legs over his waist.

Euclid laughed softly and nipped at the crest of Halcyon's breast. He brought his hips down closer and followed Halcyon's silent plea. Halcyon allowed the charade further until she felt him deep enough in her. She bit her lips against her frustrated breath and dug her nails into his back.

Thora was breathing hard, and her heart pounded against her chest. She wished to sink into the wall and vanish from the room. Once before, in Athens, she had been a witness to another sexual encounter between three Greeks. Thora only prayed she was not requested to join, much like the last time.

Cesare watched on without care. He had watched many times in the past. Thora's uneasiness went unbeknownst to him.

Thora's attention was drawn to the blood on Euclid's side. Somehow, Halcyon had caused it. She was almost certain Euclid would react poorly. Slowly, Thora's memories from last night filled her. Halcyon looked just as trapped as Thora had been. Her stomach tightened, and she struggled with her angry emotions.

Halcyon turned her head to the right, and she caught the expression on Thora's face. She had seen Thora angry many times before this, but Thora was enraged now. Halcyon was certain what had transpired last night between Euclid and Thora. She let out a low growl and suddenly rolled her body to the left. Euclid was startled and lost his dominant position.

His features darkened, and he opened his mouth to protest. However, he was silenced by Halcyon's kiss. Within beats, he lost control as Halcyon rocked her hips against him.

Thora watched her owner control her husband from her position on top. She dropped her head again and slowly, her rage ebbing about last night.

Cesare glanced at Thora and sensed her mixed emotions. Cesare dared to stretch out his left hand and touch Thora's arm. He held her arm as he hollowly stared at Halcyon dominating Euclid.

Euclid grew louder, and he matched his wife's movements. Halcyon leaned back, her eyes closed, and her mind placed her somewhere else. She quickened the pace and pleased her husband faster. Euclid's hands held his wife's hips. He helped rock her against him harder.

Halcyon's lips voiced no pleasure. She hastened the motions in hopes to end their intimacy sooner. She was relieved by Euclid's messy orgasm. She dismounted and bestowed him a quick kiss and a fake smile.

"Thora, is my bath ready?"

Thora was frozen, other than her eyes going from Euclid to Halcyon.

"Go check it for me." Halcyon freed Thora from the room, the smell, and especially the sight. She then ordered Cesare to collect a clean chiton for her and take it to the bath.

Halcyon had retrieved her red *exomis* near her armor and gazed over at Euclid. "I will see you for the last meal." She was happy to leave Euclid after performing her wifely duty.

Euclid had just caught his breath after the frantic, uncontrolled intimacy. He attempted to reply, but Halcyon was already gone.

After donning her tunic, Halcyon went downstairs into the courtyard. She passed the supply room where Glauce was preparing the evening meal. She entered the bathing room and saw Thora pour another bucket of hot water. Thora set the bucket aside and went to the open doors. Just as she was about to seal them, Cesare arrived with a chiton. Thora took it then closed the doors after Cesare left.

Halcyon disrobed from her dirty tunic, then descended the stone steps into the small bath that was large enough for three people. She moaned at the warm water that soothed her tense, strained muscles. Slowly, the lilac scent eased her mind.

Collecting her owner's favorite soap, Thora sat beside the edge of the bath, next to her owner, and placed the soap on top of the drying linen.

"Your Greek has improved," Halcyon said. She closed her eyes and leaned her head against the stone wall of the bath, near Thora.

"Yes... thank you." Thora studied Halcyon's relaxed features, deciding their private moment was her best chance to make a request. "Yarikh wishes that I learn to read and write as well."

Opening her eyes, Halcyon twisted her head and peered up at Thora. It was unheard of that a slave could read, much less write. "Has he taught you how?"

Thora shook her head. "No." She failed to tell that Yarikh had gone to the agora to purchase parchment and fresh ink for his *kalamos*. "He not told to teach me." But Yarikh planned to show her the basics, in secret. Regardless, Thora hoped that Halcyon would agree to formal lessons.

"Do you wish to learn?" Halcyon posed. She had been schooled at a young age on how to read and write. Rarely did women learn such skills, but Halcyon's father had deemed it necessary after his wife passed away so early. Halcyon stood to inherit her father's fortune, and the skills behooved her. Furthermore, Sparta encouraged women's education.

Thora gave a low nod. "*Já.*"

Halcyon turned her gaze away, hiding her smile at Thora's habit to switch between Norsk and Greek tongue. Gradually, the smile fell away as she thought about the request. In truth, Halcyon admitted if Thora could read and write, it would integrate her further into Spartan society. "Then, if that is what you wish, Yarikh shall teach you."

Thora stared in awe and nearly asked why her wish was granted to her but held back, simply saying, "Thank you."

"*Ekki at þakka,*" Halcyon replied in Thora's native tongue.

Thora wistfully smiled at Halcyon's willingness to learn some of her language. It warmed her that her owner made an attempt to speak Norsk and yet caused Thora to miss her homelands. She reached for the soap and held it out to Halcyon.

Opening her eyes, Halcyon sniffed the soap's distinct scent and took it. She lathered her body, then returned the soap to Thora's larger hand.

Thora wetted her hands and waited until Halcyon was seated in the bath again. It took nearly two months after Halcyon purchased her for them to garner enough trust that Halcyon allowed Thora to clean her hair. Halcyon put her head underwater for a moment and came up again, then long fingers started working the soap through her black tresses.

Since coming to Sparta, Thora noticed many women had shoulder length hair, but it was the younger women, like Selene, who had long hair to her mid-back. Thora concluded unmarried women in Sparta kept their hair long, while the married ones had short hair between their chin and to just past their shoulders.

Halcyon's hair had indeed been quite long after growing it since childhood. The day of her marriage, her hair was cut off, and Euclid came to her to consummate their marriage. From that day forward, Halcyon wore her hair just past her shoulders.

Halcyon accidentally moaned when Thora hit a strained muscle at her neck. She had pulled it during her time at the barracks. She was surprised when Thora massaged the strained muscle and bent her head forward for better access. Nobody had paid attention to her body's needs in the past.

Thora withdrew her hand and softly said, "You are worn from being gone."

Halcyon knew that Thora meant her training at the barracks. "It is my duty." She sank under the water and rinsed the soap from her hair.

Thora stood up with the soap and returned it to the wooden shelf on the wall, placing it in the proper spot beside the other two soaps. She looked at Halcyon, who climbed the steps out of the bath. Thora retrieved the linen and approached with it.

Halcyon was offered the linen, but for the first time, she pushed it back into Thora's hands. "You." For once, she was too tired to do the work herself.

Releasing a low breath, Thora nodded and unfolded the linen then proceeded to dry Halcyon. It was the first time she had such a close view of Halcyon's muscular body. She also counted at least eight distinct scars, one being deep on Halcyon's right shoulder. The scars whispered stories about the former battles, and Thora's respect grew for her owner.

Halcyon opened her eyes after Thora finished drying her body and her hair. Thora collected the clean chiton and helped Halcyon into it. Last, they put on the girdle around her waist.

"*Þakka fyrir,*" Halcyon softly offered.

Thora smiled at the thank you and nodded. "*Ekki at þakka.*"

Halcyon was a few hands shorter than Thora. She found it suitable as she had to gaze up at the blue sky, much like she did into Thora's eyes. Eventually, her attention was drawn down to Thora's discolored neck. Again, she touched the angry skin.

Swallowing hard, Thora wished to ask about earlier, in the bedroom, but bit down her questions for once. Now was a bad time because Halcyon was exhausted and obviously still bitter about Euclid's mistreatment.

After picturing the possible fight between Thora and Euclid, a slow burn started in Halcyon's stomach and climbed into her chest. She took personal offense to the fact her husband damaged her slave, especially when Thora was innocent of the fire. To add to it, Halcyon viewed Thora as her slave, solely. She ruled the finances and property in the marriage.

Thora saw Halcyon's bitter expression and collected the smaller hand into hers. For the first time, she felt the renewed calluses in Halcyon's palm. "It is done," she said, hoping to close the door on the past.

Halcyon sighed and freed her hand. "You are correct." She moved toward the door. "Come." There was much to do tonight before sunset, when Halcyon would start her duty shift as the king's guard. At first light, her husband would leave for the barracks, and this evening's dinner was her only social event with him.

Heeding the command, Thora carried the damp linen and the dirty tunic; both needed to be cleaned now.

Halcyon stepped out of the bathing room and into the courtyard. She cast a glance over her shoulder at Thora, who turned left. As Thora walked toward the steps to the second floor, she met Halcyon's gaze. For a brief instant, she and Halcyon held a silent conversation of understanding before they parted ways. Thora had indeed missed Halcyon's presence and was glad her owner had returned home.

CHAPTER EIGHT

Halcyon dug her nails into the dory's wood and released a worried sigh as the public meeting continued in the *bouleuterion*. She feared the outcome of the discussions, especially for her king's safety. With a roll of her shoulders, she adjusted the bronze armor that clung to her sticky body. Even without her helmet, she was still warm under the early morning sunlight. Only moments ago she had completed her evening rotation as the king's bodyguard and looked forward to going home, especially with Euclid gone. However, her king requested she joined him at the bouleuterion.

"We must act quickly," King Leonidas urged the council. Like Halcyon, he stood on the stage before the seated elders, who were fanned out in the bouleuterion. Higher up were women of various ages and stature in society.

One elder, Dromeus, rose from his seat and said, "As you know, my king, it is the second day of the Carnea Festival.

We would be smote by god Carnus, and even Apollo, if we engaged in any war activities during this sacred time."

Leonidas toyed with a ruffle in his chiton, an agitated tell of his deteriorating mood. He parted his lips, and biting words almost left his mouth until a soft hand eased him. He looked at his wife and silently conceded to her.

Queen Gorgo removed her touch and smiled at the elders. "Yes, the festival's laws are of utmost importance to all." She folded her hands in front of her. "And so is the safety of Sparta."

Dromeus was still on his feet. He often spoke for the whole of the council and continued to do so quite freely. "My queen, we do greatly appreciate the information you revealed from the tablets that Demaratus sent us, but we cannot act until after the festival."

"But we can prepare," Gorgo said.

Dromeus hesitated at the idea, but he heard agreeing murmurs from either side of him.

"We can prepare our men," Gorgo continued louder, gaining favor with both the elders and the women above them. "Because Xerxes will come here... to Sparta... to our homes. And we cannot rely on Thrace or Corinth or even Athens to stop him."

Leonidas shifted in his sandals as the elders whispered amongst each other. The tide was slightly turning in his favor, but it was hardly enough. He feared that waiting nearly a fortnight would mean Sparta's end. From months ago, he recalled the warning from the Oracle at Delphi about his future, and he realized it was about to come true. To his right, he exchanged a glance with Halcyon and made a final choice.

"Until then, I and my three hundred hippeis will march north and meet King Xerxes and his army in battle."

For several heartbeats, a silence loomed in the bouleuterion. Then a chorus of questions and demands fell from the elders. Many rose to their feet, but it was the women's claps from the back of the bouleuterion that overwhelmed the council's voice.

Gorgo studied her husband and read the determination in his hard features, knowing there were no words that would change his mind. She understood his duty as both a king and a hoplite, and she would honor his decision.

After much of the clamor subsided, Dromeus made a final attempt to disarm the king's suicidal plans. He turned his full attention to the silent hippeus, Halcyon, beside the king and asked, "And will the Iron Edge march with her king?"

"With honor," Halcyon declared with finality.

* * *

Waking up sharply, Thora sensed the morning was late and glanced about the empty room, realizing Glauce was gone. The window's mat gleamed with morning sunlight. She jumped from her bedroll and pulled off the mat for more light. The sunrise had passed a while ago, and Thora rushed to get into her chiton, cursing several times. Her heartbeat matched her speed.

Once out of the room, Thora heard voices down in the courtyard. She recognized her owner's voice, and she silently cursed again. Thora cringed, rushed to the stairs, and started down to the courtyard. Instantly, green eyes turned to Thora as she descended the steps. Halcyon's voice faded away after Thora approached her and Yarikh.

Yarikh peered up and was somewhat smug, but he turned serious after Halcyon spoke.

"Thora, you are late." An amused note hung in Halcyon's tone. She wore her red tunic, still not fully changed from her guard duty.

Remaining calm, Thora gazed down at them, as they were seated on the bench beside the pool. "I... slept not well," she said dejectedly.

Halcyon was studying Thora's features, which were indeed dark. Lately, Thora had dealt with a lot, especially the incident with Euclid. She tilted her head. "You have been busy."

Thora's attention flickered to Yarikh, who was keenly interested in Halcyon's words.

"Perhaps it would be best if you tutored this morning, Yarikh." Halcyon turned toward him, at her right. "If you do not mind."

"Of course." Yarikh dipped his head in agreement.

Halcyon gazed up at Thora. "Then you can cook only the last meal for the day."

Thora was confused by the reduced duties, expecting to be punished, not rewarded.

"Tomorrow you can continue as normal," Halcyon said, as she stood up and looked at Yarikh. "We will complete our discussion this evening." She then started toward the nearly rebuilt kitchen, but she paused and looked over her shoulder. "Thora, my husband returned to the barracks last night." She vanished into the kitchen, which needed her attention.

* * *

For the day, Yarikh and Thora practiced Greek in the courtyard. At some point, Halcyon and Cesare briefly passed by and left the villa through the front gate. Thora had seen her leave, but she stayed focused on Yarikh's lesson. About midday, Glauce brought them a plate of food to share. Just before sunset, Yarikh ended the lesson and allowed Thora to continue her chores.

In the supply room, Thora assisted Glauce with making the meal. They had learned how to work well together after Glauce picked up on a few cooking skills from Thora. Cesare shortly entered to help.

"The Persians are savages," Glauce told Thora.

"Savages?" Thora repeated, having yet to learn the word.

While organizing the new *choes* of wine from the agora, Cesare looked over at the women and explained, "Animals."

Thora glanced over her shoulder at Cesare before she plucked one of many dried herbs hanging from above her head, preparing the gyro. "Like a Norsk," she said. "Like me."

Cesare chuckled and came over to the pair. "Persians come from Hades. I do not believe a Norsk does so."

Thora grinned at him and replied, "It is cold in my lands. Hades could not live there."

Cesare mirrored her grin, then he became serious. "Why do you talk about the Persians?" He glanced at Glauce, who was arranging grapes, cheese, and bread on a plate.

"Glauce said there is war."

"That there will be war," Glauce said. "They will not speak or declare war with the Carnea Festival." Today the agora buzzed with excitement, thanks to the festival dedicated to Carnus and Apollo. Glauce set the vine of grapes down on the table and turned to the other slaves. "When I was in the agora, there was talk that word came from the former king, Demaratus, that the King of Persia marches toward Greece."

"Demaratus! That treacherous king," Cesare said with venom and huffed. "This morning, I was at the bouleuterion with Halcyon." He noted Thora's questioning glance. "The building where the city council meets, beside the agora."

Thora understood and returned to the gyros, remembering the councilmen, citizens, women, and the like collected at the bouleuterion several times.

Cesare thought back to today's council at the bouleuterion. "Demaratus sent two blank tablets to Sparta." It was those very tablets that spurred today's early morning meeting at the bouleuterion, and Cesare had patiently waited for his owner.

"That is strange," Glauce said.

Cesare shook his head. "Queen Gorgo figured out they were not, in fact, blank. There was wax concealing his warning message about the King of Persia coming into Greece."

Glauce gasped and asked, "He is here already?"

"In Thrace." Cesare was concerned by the news too.

Thora had a rough idea of Thrace's location in the northern part of Greece. Recently, Yarikh was teaching her about maps and started with Greece. She set the four gyros onto a plate and looked at the other slaves. "Will Greece fight?"

"Of course." Glauce was sure of it yet Cesare had a worried look.

"But only after the festival." Cesare remembered the arguments at the bouleuterion today. "It is sacrilegious to fight during the festival," he told Thora. "Plus Sparta must first spread word, but with the Olympiad..."

Thora frowned at what the Spartan festival or games in Olympia had to do with anything.

Glauce sighed heavily and looked at Thora. "The games are important."

Thora went slack jaw. "More than war?"

Cesare picked up a heavy oinochoe. "Sparta will rally her hoplites before the King of Persia can march any farther south into Greece." At today's meeting, Cesare heard the vote given that King Leonidas would take his three hundred guards to meet the King of Persia. Along the way, he was expected to have support from other small bands of hoplites along the Peloponnese.

Emotionally struck, Thora realized that such hoplites included Halcyon. "Ěra will fight."

Cesare touched Thora's arm and comforted her. "She is a hippeus, a very special hoplite to the king and guards him. They call her the Iron Edge because she is strong like iron and sharply skilled like the edge of a dory."

Glauce studied Thora's lost features after their owner's fate sank into Thora. "I heard the story that she stopped an assassination attempt on the king."

Cesare recalled that day from years ago when Halcyon had stayed overnight in the palace to further guard the king. Once she had returned home, Cesare had worried over the wound to Halcyon's chest that left a scar along her collarbone. After a sigh, he said, "That is when she earned the name the Iron Edge."

Thora had a thick frown as she listened to the other two slaves.

Cesare understood Thora's fears, but it was far beyond their hands. He tightened his grip on Thora's arm and asked, "Is the food ready?"

Thora refocused on the present and nodded. "Is ěra back?"

"Yes, she is in the andron with Yarikh." Cesare started to the open door with the oinochoe in hand.

Taking the plate of gyros, Thora signaled for Glauce to follow her, and they went to the andron, passing Cesare on their way. Thora placed the food on a table and took the plate from Glauce, setting it down too. Glauce handed each a bowl, then took Thora's side and waited for any other orders.

Halcyon looked directly at Glauce. "You may go and eat."

Glauce bowed her head and quietly left the andron. Thora remained standing in front of the two klines that were occupied by Yarikh and Halcyon. She was thankful it was her tutor rather than Selene.

"Yarikh and I have discussed your continued education," Halcyon said.

Yarikh was enjoying the grapes and listened to the conversation.

"We have made an arrangement for Yarikh to remain here longer and teach you to read and write." Halcyon shifted on the kline.

Thora kept her eyes trained on Halcyon. "Thank you, ĕra."

Halcyon slightly bowed her head at the gratitude. "Yarikh must return home in two to three months from now, no later." She sensed that Thora understood her enough. "You must learn quickly." Already they were into the first month of the new year and quickly approaching the second.

Thora nodded and glanced once at her tutor before she looked at Halcyon again. "Will Yarikh be back?"

"I am afraid not," Yarikh replied.

Sighing softly, Thora had to learn as much as possible before her opportunity was gone. She was thankful that Yarikh had started the reading and map lessons today.

"More of your chores will be taken over by Glauce until Yarikh returns home." Halcyon saw the pending protest so she cut it off. "Unless you wish not to learn and remain an uneducated slave, like the others."

Thora snapped her jaw shut after the warning, knowing she could easily sabotage her own wishes if she concerned herself with the chores. Indeed, Glauce could handle them for another two months. Thora silently promised to repay Glauce at a later time. "Yes, ĕra."

"Excellent. Now go eat before it is any later." From the corner of her eye, Halcyon watched Thora leave the andron. She popped a few more grapes in her mouth and continued talking with Yarikh.

* * *

As the evening wore on, everyone retired to their rooms. Thora slept rather restlessly and tossed around on her bedroll. Her mind was on her owner's future as a hoplite going into battle against the Persians. She dreamed about her owner being killed by a snarling, ugly Persian, and it woke her very early in the morning. She remained upright in her shared bedroom, hand against her sweaty chest.

Then voices from the courtyard carried up to her room. Thora slowly recognized Halcyon's deep timber followed by Cesare's reply. She was unsure what they said, only that Cesare was given an order. Thora climbed out of her bedroll and hastily put on a chiton and sandals. This morning eerily reminded her of the same morning when her owner returned to the barracks.

In the courtyard, Cesare unlatched the gate and drew it open. He sadly studied Halcyon, who was fully garbed in hoplite armor and carried her dory and *aspis*. At her back, her rucksack held a few personal items, and the helmet was tied to it. Her xiphos's hilt shone at her hip.

Cesare was about to offer prayers, until footsteps caught his attention. Twisting his head toward the steps, he spotted Thora coming down and bit his lower lip because her expression was openly distraught.

Halcyon turned to Thora, and her grip tightened on the dory. Even in the low light, Halcyon's bronze armor shined, but it would soon be painted in blood and match the red *chlamys* hooked to her shoulders. As Thora drew closer, she opened her mouth, but Cesare cut her off.

"You should be resting." Cesare stiffened when fiery blue eyes settled on him, making him guilty for withholding Halcyon's departure from Thora. He realized how imposing Thora's height could be when she made use of it.

Halcyon released a low breath, then softly said, "Leave us, Cesare." She kept her eyes on Thora and waited until Cesare was nearly gone from the courtyard.

"You leave for war."

"Yes." Halcyon moved her left arm so that the aspis was not between them. She could hardly explain to Thora how King Leonidas chose to stand against King Xerxes. Halcyon had hoped for a better strategy than three hundred hippeis and a small force of untrained men battling for time until Greece could rally all the hoplites. However, it was a better strategy than standing aside so that Xerxes's army could arrive at Sparta's unprepared doorstep. Halcyon had asserted her allegiance to King Leonidas yesterday in the bouleuterion. Such a discussion was a difficult one to have with Thora.

"You will die." Through the night, Thora had pictured it several times in her dreams. "You must not go."

"And if I do not, then Persia will come here, to this home." Halcyon indicated the courtyard and the rooms around it. "They will take all that I possess." She tilted her head and said sadly, "Including you."

"Then we do not stay here."

Halcyon balked at the idea of running from her enemy. Since childhood, she was trained to face danger and odds without restraint or fear. "I am Spartan." She hardened under the sheer foolishness. "It is my duty." Ending the conversation, Halcyon started out of the gate until a strong hand held her shoulder, pulling her back.

"Nei!" Thora held tightly to Halcyon and asked, "And your duty to your home?" She ignored Halcyon's heightened anger. "Your duty to your slaves?"

Halcyon shrugged off Thora's hold. "I will have none of those duties if they are taken from me."

"Your life is of no value? It means... to me." Thora's Greek was crumbling under her surge of emotions.

Halcyon breathed deeply, which diffused the storm in her. It was obvious they would remain at odds. Thora hardly understood her calling as a hoplite. In Thora's mind, Halcyon's life outweighed Sparta's freedom from Persia. It was a topic that Halcyon had no luxury to face right now. She was bound to her honor and aspis.

"I will return," Halcyon said proudly and saw a tide of hope in Thora's beautiful eyes. However, she destroyed it with her next promise. "I will return with my shield — or upon it." She finally turned and continued out of the gate with the weapons, armor, and aspis that made her a hoplite.

Thora stepped through the one open gate and watched Halcyon travel down the quiet street in the first light of dawn. She fisted her hands against the thunder in her heart. It was out of her control, and she could barely express her thoughts to Halcyon. If she had done so, she doubted it would have changed Halcyon's mind.

Once Halcyon's receding figure vanished, Thora backed into the courtyard. She drew the gate closed with her, then bitterly rammed the lock through to seal the gate again. Thora leaned her head against the iron bars and struggled with her emotions. She slammed a palm against a bar and softly cursed in her native tongue.

Returning, Cesare carefully approached Thora and consoled her with a one-arm hug. She tensed until she sensed that it was Cesare. Thora dropped her hands from the gate and faced the elder slave, who had slowly become a friend.

She parted her lips, about to say something, but she let her words die on her tongue.

Like Thora, Cesare had no words that could ease her pain. He denied any hollow promises that their owner would return to them. He knew that King Leonidas and the three hundred hippeis would face thousands of Persian soldiers in Thermopylae. Yesterday at the bouleuterion, he heard the king's very vow to take death if it meant victory. Cesare simply prayed that Halcyon's body would be returned to them rather than desecrated by the Persians.

Cesare's only comfort to Thora was to draw her into his arms, holding her close and allowing her to work through the pain.

Thora was thankful for Cesare's understanding as they hugged for some time. She was furious that Halcyon left them, upset her Greek was still weak, and scared about her future after seeming to find a stable home with Halcyon. The Fates were cruel, and Thora despised them for the life given to her.

CHAPTER NINE

Today was the first battle against King Xerxes and his vengeful army. Over six thousand Greek hoplites held a blockade at the pass outside of Thermopylae against hundreds of thousands of beastly Persians. Similarly, the strait near Artemisium was being blocked by four hundred Greek triremes, who faced over a thousand ships from Persia.

King Leonidas and his three hundred hippeis were hoplites descended from Heracles. On Thermopylae's beach, they became the impenetrable wall that blocked Xerxes's raging flood until the rest of the Greek city-states could rally to arms. They would not allow Persia to take Greece and their freedom.

King Xerxes only withdrew his men for a few hours in the night, after thousands were killed by the small Greek force. This gave Leonidas a chance to conjure up more creative ways to hold his enemy at bay. It also allowed his hippeis a chance to rest, clean their wounds, and eat before Apollo brought the sun over the eastern horizon.

One of Leonidas's injured hoplites was being tended to by a comrade, Olus. Leonidas had found his injured hoplite beside a campfire, and he was highly concerned. Over a fortnight ago, they had arrived in Thermopylae and planned for Xerxes's army. The journey from Sparta had taken many days and tired his men. However, the original three hundred hoplites had amassed to over six thousand once they arrived in Thermopylae, many poleis pledging hoplites to the cause.

However, during the slow trip north to Thermopylae, Leonidas noticed that his finest hippeus became weaker by the day. Each morning, she was bent over the nearest bush, and today, she was injured due to her slowed reaction. He made every attempt to convince the injured hippeus to return to Sparta. However, he feared that Halcyon would not listen to him.

Halcyon continued staring straight ahead, past the campfire. She never flinched as her fellow hoplite stitched the sword wound on her right shoulder. She deserved the wound for being slow and weak. Her bronze armor did its best, but it failed to fully break the barbarian's strike during today's battle. She gritted her teeth against the memory of her failure but relished killing the Persian barbarian once she recovered from her error.

But it was that particular mistake which was personally costing her the war now. Halcyon blinked against the persistent sting in her left eye. She had washed the blood from her face, yet it still bothered her. The laceration on her brow was at least dry now. She slowly fisted her hands while the Spartan king continued speaking reason to her. Her fire-lit eyes flickered up to Leonidas.

"You must go, Halcyon." Leonidas declined ordering her, although he felt he might have to if she disagreed further with him. "It is important you live." His rich brown eyes lifted and scanned over the littered battlefield along the coastline. "There is no chance of survival here."

Halcyon was quiet for a long moment. "I am a hippeus," she said coldly, bitter features locked on the campfire.

Leonidas reached down and gently touched his hippeus's uninjured shoulder. "And one of my finest — until the Fates told us you are now carrying the future." He tilted his head and lowered his hand. "Sparta's future." He saw that Halcyon refused to believe in his words. "There is no Sparta without hoplites."

Olus had stitched up Halcyon and finished wrapping her shoulder wound. With his minor training in healing, he was able to care for Halcyon's injury, but it still needed an expert eye. After a moment, he noticed the king's continued silence, and Olus was tempted to speak up, until he decided against it.

Halcyon kept the arguments silent, loathing the king's wishes and cursed her own fate. Above all, she hated her weak, female body that had done nothing but displease her since she left Sparta nearly a month ago. Once her shoulder was finished, she stood up and left the small camp without a word.

Leonidas left well enough alone, for now. However, he went in search of his commander, who was eating his tasteless dinner. He spoke with Stesichoros about removing Halcyon before first light, and while Stesichoros understood the king's wishes, he disliked forcibly stripping Halcyon of her honor to return to Sparta. He promised Leonidas that Halcyon would be cared for, only if she agreed to go back to Sparta. Leonidas admired Stesichoros's middle ground loyalty to both him and Halcyon.

After the discussion, the king decided on a final attempt with Halcyon. He easily tracked her down just beyond the campgrounds along the beach, grateful for the darkness because it hid the bloody sand and water. The mess of Persian bodies, broken weapons, and impaled arrows forced him to walk slower. The king inhaled the refreshing salt air that drifted off the sea, after he came up to the lone hoplite.

Halcyon drew her red chlamys around her weak body, once the king was at her side. She barely acknowledged him with a look and stared at the sea. The waves' constant washing onto the shore seemed to ease away her earlier anger about today.

"You are not a failure, Halcyon. There is no dishonor in this." Leonidas grew quiet and listened to the waves peacefully brushing against the sandy shoreline, a stark difference compared to the cries and pains of war on the beach earlier today.

Halcyon shook her head once and quietly said, "The gods have cursed me."

Leonidas turned his wide-eyed expression to her. "The gods have given you nothing but gifts in your life, including this one."

"Not this one." Halcyon finally met the king's gaze. "It has weakened me. I am half the hoplite I should be."

"You are more than one hoplite now," Leonidas replied, sternly but with a plea in his eyes. "And that is what you must remember over these coming months." He gingerly touched Halcyon's arm. "I am proud of you, Halcyon. I must know your life will continue." He turned to her and now cupped her flushed cheeks. "Go home, for me."

Halcyon searched the aged king's eyes. Over time, she had come to care deeply for the king, and he had become a father to her. She had been one of his hippeis for many years now, and she hated to be away from his side during battle.

"Please, Halcyon," Leonidas whispered.

Halcyon bowed her head into her king's warm hands. "Very well."

Leonidas was truly relieved and kissed Halcyon's temple, over the battle wound. "Thank you." He withdrew his hands. "Come to camp with your brothers."

Halcyon silently conceded because this was her last time with them. Her heart was heavy now that she had made her choice to return to Sparta, alone. Once back in the meager camp, she indeed bonded with her brothers throughout the night, until Stesichoros fetched her. She swore to her brothers that their song would be told back in Sparta. Halcyon then shared a long hug with Leonidas and accepted a folded message meant for Gorgo.

"Be safe on your journey home," Leonidas said.

Halcyon withdrew from the hug, but she left her hands on her king's padded shoulders, gazing deep into his earthy-brown eyes. "I will see you soon."

"Yes. Upon my shield." Leonidas had accepted his fate months ago and looked forward to his foretold destiny. "Please tell my wife that I love her."

Nodding, Halcyon pressed her left palm against the king's bristly cheek, leaned in, and softly kissed his other cheek. "I will not forget you, my king." She straightened up and turned to Stesichoros, who returned her dory and aspis.

"Two Thespian hoplites will escort you home," Stesichoros told Halcyon on the walk to the rear of the camp. He paused when Halcyon looked back at the camp, then followed her gaze back at the hippeis, who swore to protect Leonidas as his honorable guardians.

Halcyon was saddened at her brothers' future deaths, but they would be honorable.

"Halcyon, dawn is quickly approaching." Stesichoros knew how hard it was for Halcyon to leave her post, comrades, and king during what would most likely be the darkest, yet most inspiring, battle in Spartan history. It would haunt Halcyon for many months.

Forcing herself to turn away, Halcyon shoved on her helmet, which had blood spots, dents, and a tear on the backside. She left the camp with Stesichoros and sought out the Thespians, who waited for her at the pass.

Stesichoros called out to them. They glowed under the moonlight thanks to their bronze armor. They were welcoming to Halcyon and swore to Stesichoros that they would see her home. Stesichoros was grateful, and he exchanged a heartfelt farewell with his comrade.

Halcyon hefted her dory as the Thespians took her side. She gave a final nod to Stesichoros and left with the Thespians, heading south for Sparta.

Stesichoros remained there until Halcyon and the Thespians were gone from view. "May the gods protect you." He faced the camp and started back to his brothers.

* * *

It was a long journey back to Sparta, even longer than the journey from Sparta. Halcyon was unsure if the trip would come to an end. Her declining health made matters difficult and slow. She refused to acknowledge her ailments to her companions, although Stesichoros had told them.

Nearly every morning, Halcyon would steal away from the camp until she had space from the Thespians. Then she would finally crumble to her knees behind a tree or rock and allow her last meal to burn against her throat until there were only dry heaves. The stench under her nose was revolting and made her loathe her body further.

After several gulps of air, Halcyon would rinse her mouth and calmly return to camp. She would choke down a breakfast and prayed it would remain in her stomach. What made matters worse was her shoulder wound swelled, and foul pus oozed from it. Her armor constantly scraped the wound and irritated it further. Halcyon sensed a fever come over her a few days after leaving Thermopylae. The late summer's heat added to her body's stress. She sternly reminded herself she was a hoplite and continued the march to Sparta.

The Thespian hoplites spoke little during the trip south. Everyone silently shared concerns for the battles at Thermopylae and Artemisium. The Thespians knew they would return to the war but after the battle in the pass ended. They sensed that Leonidas and his hippeis would not survive the bloody battle for many more days. Even for three hundred Spartans, it was impossible to hold off King Xerxes's infinite lust for revenge. But by then, the games would conclude, and the Spartan army would mobilize for battle.

Halcyon was plagued by guilt for leaving her king's side and her brothers, her return to Sparta felt like a true failure. She could only imagine what fellow hoplites in Sparta would think of her, so she attempted to think about other things, like her home.

As such thoughts passed, she wondered how Thora was faring now. A full month and several days would have passed by the time Halcyon returned home. Thora's Greek would have improved further since her departure. She had reminded Yarikh to continue schooling her each day as well as look after Thora's interests. Admittedly, Halcyon had secretly grown protective over her Norsk slave, but she disliked if people saw it. Yarikh had lightly brushed the topic with her, and she nearly cancelled her arrangements with him. Yarikh apologized rather sincerely and remained silent about Halcyon and Thora's unusual relationship.

As Halcyon drew closer to Sparta, she actually looked forward to seeing her home where peace waited for her. She imagined the olive trees along the street to her house, and she could almost smell the blossoms. At the villa's open gate, Cesare would be there with his loyal, warm smile in place. Then Thora would stroll into the courtyard and wipe her hands on a linen towel from the kitchen. In her imaginings, Thora was surrounded by a sweet air from baking. Halcyon returned Cesare's smile but reached out and gently touched Thora's pale cheek.

Instead, Halcyon hit a stone with her foot and nearly toppled forward, but her dory caught her. Her warm vision of home drifted away and left Halcyon's skin hot and heart chilly. She was far from home, despite her longing. Like the Thespians, she hoped to be in Sparta within a day and a half, yet the distance seemed incredibly long to her.

After they stopped to make camp, Halcyon repacked her shoulder wound with salt. She noted the wound had split open wider, but she could do nothing for it. She ate little and nearly collapsed into her bedroll, once her fever spiked for the day. Thankfully, the cool night aided her overheated body that battled against the infection from her shoulder. By dawn, the Thespians roused her, and she mustered all her strength to put on her armor and pick up her aspis.

One Thespian attempted to take Halcyon's aspis, but he was denied by the tip of the dory at his face. He warily backed off from the ailing Spartan and considered whether she would make it home. He prayed the female hoplite's pride kept her more alive than dead.

* * *

By the following day, the weary travelers finally approached the fields that surrounded Sparta. Halcyon recognized the lands immediately, and her pace increased although her body was nearly to its end. The Thespians recommended they go to the barracks and find a healer. Halcyon ignored their ideas and instead went directly home after entering the city gates. She barely registered all the onlookers' strange and curious gazes. The Thespians remained at the hippeus's side until she slowed near the entrance to a villa.

Halcyon's dory had become a crutch as she entered her home's courtyard. She leaned heavily against the dory, and suddenly, her aspis felt like a rock tied to her. She attempted to call for her slaves, but her throat was dry. Already, the Thespians' entrance had roused the slaves.

Cesare came out of the supply room after he had helped Glauce put certain items away from the agora. He stared wide-eyed at his owner's unexpected return.

"By the gods!" Thora was in awe after she entered the courtyard from the rebuilt kitchen. She hastened across the courtyard to her owner, who was about to collapse. One Thespian moved forward, but he halted when the tall, unusual slave jumped forward first.

Thora caught Halcyon, but she remained bent forward because Halcyon was so heavy with the armor and weapons. "Cesare, remove her aspis."

Halcyon dropped her dory, which clanked loudly against the courtyard's stone floor.

Breaking from his stupor, Cesare freed the aspis, lowered it to the ground, and watched as Thora moved her right arm under Halcyon's bent legs. Thora clenched her teeth as she lifted up and adjusted the fallen hoplite in her arms. She let the bronze helmet slide off, and it loudly hit the ground to reveal Halcyon's stricken features. It had been years since Thora had seen someone so close to death. After lifting Halcyon more, a horrible wound peeked out from under the armor.

"She is injured," Thora told the other slaves. "You must retrieve the healer."

Cesare rushed out of the open gate.

Thora ignored the two hoplites. "Glauce." She startled the girl, who was staring at Halcyon. "Boil a pot of water."

Glauce ran across the courtyard to the kitchen.

Thora exchanged a glance with the two hoplites but said nothing, too panicked by Halcyon's injuries, and a rush flooded her veins which helped her take Halcyon upstairs.

The Thespian hoplites briefly watched, then turned and left the home.

On the second floor, Thora entered the thalamus and lowered Halcyon onto the small bed. Hastily, Thora removed the xiphos, greaves, and cuirasses, then the sandals last. She left Halcyon in her red exomis and exited the room in search of supplies. Hopefully, Cesare would return soon with a healer.

Emerging from his room, Yarikh was surprised by Halcyon's return and assisted Glauce with the pot of hot water. Thora tended to Halcyon after Yarikh brought the water upstairs. Just as she finished cleaning her, a healer entered with Cesare. Thora stepped aside and prayed the healer could help their owner, who was so close to passing to the Underworld. If Halcyon died now before Thora's eyes, then even the Fates could not hide from Thora's wrath.

CHAPTER TEN

Thora remained slumped in the hard wooden chair. She had her head propped against the wall as she slept through the night. This was her second night in the same spot, although Cesare offered to keep watch on their owner. Thora refused and, instead, reclaimed her seat near Halcyon's bed.

Halcyon stirred a few hours before dawn. Her movements and cough alerted Thora, who popped up from the chair. What little candlelight was left was enough for Thora to gather a skyphos of water.

"You must drink." Thora helped Halcyon sit up and drink. She then set the clay skyphos on the small table beside the bed.

Halcyon lowered into the bed again and touched Thora's skin. "My eyes deceive me." Her voice strained from disuse.

Thora briefly gathered the smaller hand into her own. "You are home but must rest more." She pulled up the fur.

Halcyon heeded the command and instantly fell asleep. She only moaned a few times when Thora wiped her brow with a damp cloth. Thora sat in the chair again and studied the ill hoplite. The healer had treated Halcyon's injuries, and Thora expected him to return tomorrow. In the meantime, Thora took care of her. She could hardly fathom why Halcyon had returned home.

* * *

The next day, Halcyon stirred in the late morning and heard someone leave the room. She was unsure who it was until Glauce came into view. Halcyon attempted to sit up, but her shoulder flared up in pain. She groaned and slumped deeper into the bed.

"You must rest." Thora entered the room after Glauce had found her. She went to Halcyon's side and knelt down. "You must heal."

Halcyon gazed upon Thora's familiar features and felt a sense of relief. "How long?"

Thora hesitated as she tried understanding the question. "You came home three days ago this afternoon."

Halcyon wished to get up, so she started moving out of bed until Thora pressed a hand into her good shoulder.

"The healer insisted you rest more."

Halcyon shook her head. "I have slept enough." She wished to go to the barracks and report their king's plans, but her weakened body gave out under her. She doubted King Leonidas was even alive.

Thora caught her. "You are weak." She settled Halcyon onto the bed. "You should eat." She looked over her right shoulder at Glauce. "Bring the broth and bread."

Glauce nodded and disappeared from the room.

"The healer will return today," Thora said and handed a skyphos. "He is uncertain how you are still alive." Her eyes lowered to the hidden wound under her owner's shift. "Your fever broke last night."

Halcyon drank all the water, then handed the skyphos back to Thora. "You stayed here all night," she said.

Remaining silent, Thora turned when Glauce arrived with the food, took the plate, and placed it on the table. "More water, please," she ordered, then handed Halcyon the bowl of broth.

Halcyon remained seated on the side of the bed as she ate the hot meal. She loved the comforting flavors of home and thanked the gods she made it back.

"You have many cuts." Thora had inspected nearly every span of Halcyon's body. The shoulder wound was the most dangerous. Yet, the most noticeable one was the cut on Halcyon's eyebrow, over her eyelid up to the top of her cheek. Yesterday, Thora examined Halcyon's helmet, which mirrored the other half of the cut at the top then down to the eye slit. She wondered whether it would leave a scar on Halcyon's beautiful face.

Halcyon ate slowly but peered up from the bowl. "Gifts from the battle." She was sore all over, especially her shoulder and right side. Most likely, she had a few broken ribs, which would simply require time to heal.

Thora let the silence pass for a moment, but her curiosity finally won, and she asked, "Why have you returned home?"

Halcyon lowered the spoon into the nearly empty bowl and placed it on the table. "I do not wish to speak of it." She tasted the bread, which added weight to her stomach.

Thora frowned and relented, for now. "Other... hoplites came to see you, but I sent them away."

Halcyon was keenly interested in the news until a wave of nausea hit her frail body.

Thora came over and said, "Lie down."

Halcyon conceded and rested on her back, placing her hands on her treacherous stomach. "Thora?"

Thora knelt beside Halcyon.

"*Þakka fyrir*," Halcyon said sincerely.

Thora sadly smiled at the gratitude and gently touched Halcyon's arm. "*Ekki at þakka.*" She went to the window. "Rest until the healer comes." With the mat in hand, she hooked it over the window, and the darkened room was only lit by the candlelight from the walls. Thora collected the bowl and allowed Glauce to return with water before their owner returned to sleep.

* * *

Shortly before sunset, Thora led Giles to Halcyon and removed the window mat for better light.

Giles spent almost an hour with Halcyon. He concluded she was on her way to recovery, but it would take time. It was obvious her wounds from battle had weakened her greatly, perhaps more than necessary. Giles left Thora with a special salve to keep Halcyon's shoulder wound clean. He doubted the salve would fail to halt any scars, including the one on her face.

Once Giles left, Halcyon requested a bath and waited for Thora to organize the proper linens and clothes. Briefly, Halcyon dozed off while Thora prepared the bathing room, and she stirred upon Thora's return.

The task to take Halcyon to the bath was slow and difficult. Halcyon insisted on walking there, but Thora kept close to her. Cesare waited at the bottom of the steps in case Halcyon lost her footing, releasing a breath when she made it down safely.

Halcyon was cautious while going through the courtyard in the darkness. As she approached the bathing room, she wondered where Yarikh was or if he had gone home.

Thora closed the door behind them and guided Halcyon to the in-ground bath. Once in front of the steps, she helped remove Halcyon's shift, then went to the stools where the linens were placed earlier.

Halcyon hesitated in front of the bath's steps, barely trusting her legs and weak body. "Thora?"

Setting the shift on the floor, Thora peered over at her weakened owner and quickly came to her. She almost asked what was wrong, until Halcyon looked at her.

Halcyon cleared her throat and said, "Bathe with me."

Thora nearly argued until she saw the concern in Halcyon's normally icy features. She nodded and took off her sandals. "Let me help you in first." Gingerly, they descended into the inviting water. Thora lifted her half-soaked chiton and slipped out of it after she organized the soap and cloth by the bath.

Halcyon enjoyed the water that soothed her injured body even though her shoulder wound stung for a while. She leaned against the wall of the bath and looked over when her nude slave approached the steps. Thora only recalled one other time when Halcyon had seen her nude body. She masked her own insecurity and hastened into the bath.

For a brief instant, Halcyon was fascinated by the delicate brown that speckled over Thora's shoulders and arms. She remained silent because it was obvious that Thora was uneasy in the bath. "Come sit by me." There was just enough room for two people to sit side by side.

Thora did so and became comfortable beside the other woman, wondering how common it was for a slave to bathe with their owner.

Leaning her head against the stone, Halcyon closed her eyes and sensed the tiredness in her limbs from the trip downstairs. Most likely, it showed on her face too. "Your Greek has improved greatly."

Thora rested against the wall, too, and stared across the room. "We are reading and writing more now."

"Good." Halcyon now knew that Yarikh was still in her home. "We have much to discuss, now that we can speak."

With a tilt of her head towards Halcyon, Thora asked, "What do we have to discuss?"

"You," Halcyon said simply and indicated the soap.

Thora retrieved it, lathered the cloth, and washed her owner, including her thick and matted hair that would require further untangling later, after Thora put oil in it. For now, the blood and grime of the kills at Thermopylae were cleaned away.

After Halcyon was done, Thora quickly bathed herself before the water grew chilly, then climbed out of the bath and obtained two drying linens from the small shelf. She hastily came to the bath's stairs just as Halcyon started up them. Thora assisted her up the steps, then dried her. Halcyon struggled with the clean shift while Thora put her still-damp chiton back on.

Once dressed, Halcyon slowly approached the sealed door, but she could barely pull on the ring. Thora jerked the door open and allowed Halcyon through first. She followed while brushing back her damp, golden strands.

As they reached the stairs, Halcyon lifted her leg to the first step, but her knees gave out under her. She fell back into Thora, who caught her easily. "Hades!"

Thora squatted and moved her arms around Halcyon, exhibiting her own hidden strength when she lifted Halcyon off the steps.

"Thora," Halcyon said with disapproval.

"No one sees." Thora and Halcyon were alone in the courtyard.

In Thora's arms, Halcyon was struck by the memory that Thora had carried her before, days ago. She shortly found herself in bed again.

"Rest," Thora said. "I will bring a meal soon." After a nod, she placed the mat over the window and silently left the room.

Nearly an hour later, Thora returned with a small plate of food and found Halcyon asleep. Glauce joined her and refilled the skyphos on the nightstand. Finally, Halcyon stirred awake and sat up in the bed.

Thora sat down after handing the food to her owner. Halcyon enjoyed the meal that Thora had made her. The dark olives were especially good with the honey. It was the first time Thora had served such a treat.

"Have you begun to write?" Halcyon asked.

Thora broke away from her thoughts. "Yes. Yarikh is a good teacher."

Halcyon considered the assessment and popped a salty-sweet olive into her mouth. "I am pleased. You have learned much in these months."

Thora bowed her head, unsure about how to reply.

Halcyon placed the dish on the table and took the filled skyphos, drinking the cool water. "Are all your people similar to you?"

"Not all."

Halcyon had a slight grin. "Perhaps taller."

Thora tilted her head at the slight tease. "Some, yes." She went to the table that had the salve and removed the wooden lid. "I must clean your wound."

Sighing, Halcyon peered over at her healing shoulder then set the skyphos on the table.

Thora carefully unwrapped the cloth after she untied it, noticing less blood than this morning on the linen. "Does it still trouble you?"

"It is fine." Halcyon hid any discomfort as Thora applied the salve, training her eyes across the room.

Thora suspected her question bothered Halcyon, but she wished to understand Halcyon's health. Instead, she had to visually inspect the wound and make her own conclusion. It appeared to be healing, and the skin had started to seal around the wound, but it would still take time. Thora retied the linen and decided it could be changed the next morning. She returned the salve and took the dirty dish. "Goodnight, ĕra," she said on her way out of the room.

Halcyon remained rigid for a beat before turning and sinking into the bed again. The candles' soft glow lulled her to sleep. Tomorrow, she swore to leave the bed, rise like normal, and tell the story about King Xerxes and King Leonidas.

CHAPTER ELEVEN

Halcyon was brought to her knees and struggled against her stomach, but it was useless as partially-digested food surged up her throat. She brought up her meal after eating it just half an hour ago. As her stomach settled, she heard hurried footsteps from outside the room. Halcyon remained seated on the wooden floor, clutching her weakened stomach, hardly surprised by Thora's arrival.

Shoving the curtain aside, Thora knelt beside her owner and demanded, "What is wrong?" From the kitchen, she had heard the fast movements from the thalamus, followed by the heaving noises.

"It is nothing." Halcyon brushed off the concerns. "Leave me." She remained seated close to the ouranē, which had been emptied recently.

Thora ignored the order and worriedly studied her owner's tired features. "You should be resting."

"I have rested plenty." Halcyon was harsh and felt guilty after a moment.

"You are hardly well." Thora placed her hand against Halcyon's forehead, but the fever was long gone. She was unsure why Halcyon was throwing up this morning. "The healer suggested-"

"I hardly give a damn," Halcyon said with a bite. She started getting to her feet, but she needed Thora's help. "I must go to the bouleuterion today." Halcyon took a deep breath and felt most of the nausea pass her.

"I will accompany you," Thora said.

Halcyon usually went alone, but at times, Cesare joined her. She nearly protested yet only had enough strength to go to the bouleuterion. "Very well."

Releasing a breath, Thora nodded once.

"We must go now." Halcyon cleared her throat. "But I need something to clear my mouth."

Starting out of the latrine, Thora promised, "I will meet you in the courtyard."

Halcyon was grateful for the moment of solitude. Breathing deeply, she put one foot in front of the other and went to the thalamus. First, she retrieved the message for

Gorgo that Leonidas had asked her to deliver for him. She then met Thora down in the courtyard and received a full skyphos that contained the mouth rinse. Thora waited until her owner was finished, then they left home through the open gate. The walk to the agora was slow, but they made it before the meeting started at the bouleuterion. They entered from the side and took a seat near the stage. Behind them, over a hundred council members and citizens sat in the stone seats that lined up the bouleuterion. It was the first time that Thora had been inside, after passing it numerous times when she went to the agora. She struggled keeping her curiosity to a minimum.

Halcyon saw Thora's interest in the amphitheatre-style building where the council held meetings for many years now. She leaned in close and quietly said, "I will speak at some point, but you must remain seated here."

Thora nodded.

Halcyon straightened up and centered her attention on the small stage as a few members gathered before the entire council. She listened to their talks about the war with King Xerxes. Occasionally, she glanced at Thora, who was rather captivated by the council meeting. She wondered if Thora's people held such councils in their villages.

"Halcyon." A beautiful woman to the side of the stage had called out to Halcyon. Her dark hair was curly and slightly longer than Halcyon's own. A beautiful golden necklace matched her arm bracelet. She smiled when Halcyon stood up.

Thora studied the beautiful woman, who had beckoned her owner. Simply from the woman's attire, Thora summarized that the woman held power in the city.

Halcyon descended the few steps and joined the council on the stage. She went directly to the beautiful woman and offered a soft apology as she gave the king's message to her. Halcyon then was instructed to speak about what had transpired in Thermopylae. She recounted the entire tale to the council. To all present, it was obvious that King Leonidas had died with his shield and with great honor. After the story, Halcyon encouraged the council to send the army, and then she returned to her seat.

After nearly half the day, the council ended with plans to immediately mobilize the army, now that the games were concluded. The march to Thermopylae would only take a handful of days. There they would meet King Xerxes head on, without any restraint.

As the councilors filtered out of the bouleuterion, Halcyon slowly climbed to her feet. Thora followed her example but noticed Halcyon's weary manner. She stayed close as they entered the aisle. Their exit was cut off by the same beautiful woman. Halcyon turned on her heels and gazed upon the woman, who climbed the steps to her. She offered a smile, but it was weak from fatigue.

"Halcyon..."

Thora shifted to the side and gazed upon the striking beauty of the newcomer and recognized her as the one who had asked Halcyon to speak to the council.

"Queen Gorgo." Halcyon gave a slight bow.

"That is unnecessary." Gorgo came up another step, which was directly below Halcyon. "I wanted to thank you for speaking to the council today."

"Of course."

Gorgo studied Halcyon's worn features. Briefly, her eyes cut to the shoulder wound that had been obtained from the battle at Thermopylae. "And I thank you for your service at Thermopylae."

Halcyon's full lips turned down. "I hardly fought, my queen, and for that, I am greatly ashamed by my return."

Gorgo reached forward and grasped Halcyon's arm, feeling the firm muscle under the skin. "My husband would not have sent you home without good cause." She had yet to learn why, but she suspected the truth would come soon.

Halcyon swallowed hard and replied, "It is my own failing."

Gorgo bit her bottom lip. "Perhaps one day soon, you will explain such to me." She finally released Halcyon.

"Perhaps." Halcyon was nearly drained from the day, which was hardly over. Apollo's chariot was at its highest point in the sky, hours still to go until darkness.

Gorgo pressed no further and instead looked to the right at the unusual slave who accompanied Halcyon.

Halcyon understood Gorgo's interest and held out her hand to Thora. "Queen Gorgo, this is my slave, Thora."

Gorgo studied the tall slave, who had light-colored hair and sharp blue eyes. She did not risk repeating the strange name, which was most likely in the slave's native tongue. She doubted the polis owned the slave, which meant she was Halcyon's personal property. "Where did you find such a slave?"

Halcyon was slightly uneasy but had known Gorgo for a long time. It was hardly a secret that Halcyon's father had made his fortunes in Athens and brought them to Sparta. After a nervous breath, she answered, "From Telamon." She suspected Gorgo was familiar with the slave trader.

Gorgo could hardly move her eyes away from Thora. "Where is she from?"

Halcyon nearly spoke with her lips parted halfway.

"I am Norsk," Thora said, proudly.

Gorgo slowly raised an eyebrow.

Halcyon gave a faint warning look to Thora but glanced at her queen again. "As you can see, she has quickly learned our language."

"Yes," Gorgo replied thoughtfully. She turned her amused features onto Halcyon. "And I can also see she has an independent spirit, like her owner."

Shifting on her feet, Halcyon simply bowed in silent request. "My queen."

Gorgo understood Halcyon's unspoken need to go. "I expect an invitation once you are well enough, Halcyon." She left her last words between them and went back down the steps.

Halcyon watched her queen leave, and she noticed Thora did the same. "Come."

As ordered, Thora followed behind.

Halcyon sensed that Thora was unnaturally close to her and most likely concerned about Halcyon's well-being. She inwardly sighed but decided it was hardly worth an argument. "What did you think of the meeting?"

Thora had a thoughtful look and replied, "It is different than the Norsk way."

Halcyon tilted her head in interest. "How so?"

"We are led by one."

Halcyon understood because Spartan culture had kings too, but they were often balanced by a council. In other Greek poleis, the government was controlled by the people.

"There is no council," Thora said.

Approaching the open gate of her home, Halcyon slowed beside the entrance to the courtyard and waited until Thora was at her side.

"It greatly intrigued me."

Halcyon heard a hint of appreciation and would again take Thora, who enjoyed the Greek culture.

Thora noticed Halcyon's worn posture. "You should rest."

"You have said that many times to me of late."

"Only out of concern," Thora said. "You have yet to heal." She eyed the shoulder wound with open worry. "I must change your dressing soon."

Halcyon was pleased by Thora's administration to her health and well-being since her return from battle. She suspected, between Giles and Thora, she recovered sooner than most. "Join me upstairs, then."

Following, Thora watched Halcyon's unsteady movements up the steps. Once in the thalamus, she found

Glauce cleaning and putting new sheets on the bed. She instructed Glauce to prepare a meal. Halcyon smiled at Thora's command over the house slaves, including Cesare. She was thankful for Thora's newfound authority over them.

Thora gingerly pushed one of the chiton's straps off Halcyon's injured shoulder. After she redressed the wound, she helped Halcyon change into a fresh night shift and asked, "Do you wish to eat here or in the andron?"

Halcyon weighed the options and replied, "In the courtyard."

Thora understood the desire to be in the courtyard where it was sunny and even calm. "I will return to wake you."

Halcyon nodded, then lowered onto the bed and fell asleep as Thora's footfalls faded away. She slept fitfully for the next few hours until Thora roused her. She went to the courtyard, and Thora emerged with several plates of food. Halcyon eyed the honey-coated olives. Thora was about to return to the kitchen, but she was halted by Halcyon.

"Join me."

Thora squinted at the strange request.

"We still have much to discuss." Halcyon noted Glauce, who arrived with the wine. "Glauce, fetch another plate and skyphos after you finish pouring my wine."

"Yes, ĕra." Glauce smiled at Thora's hesitation to take the seat next to their owner, until she was reminded to go.

Halcyon collected the bowl of honey olives and quickly popped them into her mouth. "These are very good." Thora had noticed Halcyon greatly favored the olive treat. "Have you tried them?"

Thora shook her head.

"Then you must." Halcyon handed her the bowl.

Thora was leery of the honey-coated olives, but she ate one. She blinked a few times at the salty and sweet taste that filled her mouth. Olives were a strange food compared to what her people ate in the Norsk lands. Halcyon chuckled at the startled expression. Once Glauce brought a plate and filled Thora's skyphos, Halcyon told her to leave them, wanting their discussion to remain private.

"We do not have these in Norsk." Thora pointed at the bowl of honey olives.

Halcyon placed different items on her plate. "What did you often eat?"

"We ate much fish," Thora replied. "Also cow and pig and other livestock."

"I enjoy fish," Halcyon said. "When it is affordable."

Since her enslavement, Thora had very little fish, greatly missing it.

"Are there figs in Norsk?"

Thora shook her head. "I like the fig. It's much better than the olive."

Halcyon chuckled and smiled. "I cannot imagine my life without olives."

Thora remained quiet and focused on the food. She tore up slices of bread and coated it with the olive oil and herb dip.

Halcyon sensed Thora's hidden dismay and knew it had to do with her enslavement and loss of home. She sighed. "You must miss home greatly."

Thora remained quiet as she composed her reply carefully. "I have learned to accept Greece."

Halcyon had a thin frown and sadly said, "I am afraid Greece will not fully accept you." Her cold words held only the truth.

Thora knew that Halcyon was different from the rest of the Greeks. She let her own pain ebb and remarked, "It does not have to accept me."

Halcyon silently agreed. She took a piece of bread and ate it. "Tell me what your name means."

Thora had a slight grin, which lightened her dismal features. "It is Norsk for..." She tried recalling the Greek word but was at a loss. She bit her lip and looked up to the sky. "When there is rain and light in the sky. The sound that the storm makes?"

"Thunder."

Thora had a wider grin now and nodded. "That is my name."

Halcyon smiled at the perfect name for her slave.

"And what of your name?" Thora drank some of her wine.

Halcyon shook her head. "My name means peace and calmness."

Thora choked on the wine and hastily put it on the table, coughing several times until her throat cleared itself.

"Do I amuse you?"

Thora shook her head and hoarsely replied, "I apologize, ěra."

Halcyon kept a stoic expression, but a grin broke it.

"You are a hoplite."

Halcyon shrugged and crossed her legs. "It is a slight naming error on my father's part." She remembered her father's tale about her name. "A Halcyon is a bird, who once was a woman."

Thora tilted her head.

"She had a lover named Ceyx, who had lost his brother and wished to seek him out. His lover, Halcyon, pleaded for him to stay, but Ceyx could not be dissuaded, so he boarded a ship for the journey to the Oracle of Apollo." Halcyon sipped on her wine, then held the skyphos by one of its handles in her lap. "Halcyon bid him farewell with tears."

"Did he make it to the oracle?"

Halcyon shook her head. "He did not. On the very first night, the seas were treacherous and the winds so strong. The waves lifted his ship to the gods then fell away, and his ship crashed to the bottom of the ocean." She noted Thora's continued intrigue. "Ceyx floated along the monstrous seas and cried for Halcyon to no avail until he drowned to death. The same night, Morpheus, the God of Sleep, came to Halcyon and told her of Ceyx's death."

Sighing sadly, Thora leaned back on the bench. "What happened then?"

"Halcyon raced to the cliffs and saw her lover's body had floated close to shore. With such grief, Halcyon threw herself over the cliff, but before she hit the seas, she turned into a beautiful bird." Halcyon paused and reclaimed the bowl of olives. "She flew just above the water and went to Ceyx. She collected him into her wings and cried out her grief. She tried kissing him with her beak, but it was in vain. Then the gods took pity on Halcyon and Ceyx."

Thora thought about what pity the Greek gods showed the couple.

"Ceyx was turned into the same bird, but he was still dead. Halcyon was able to take her dead lover to his burial." Halcyon went quiet for a beat. She drank more wine. "Every seven days before the Winter Solstice, Halcyon builds a floating nest on the seas and lays her eggs. After the Winter Solstice, she broods over her nest and chicks until they can fly. For a fortnight, Halcyon keeps the winds and seas calm... the calmest ever."

Thora shook her head and wondered how the name suited her owner. She tried the cheese next.

Halcyon neatly cut the lamb that Thora had cooked. "Tell me about your lands, your life before becoming a slave." She placed several pieces of lamb on a large piece of bread and handed it to Thora, who was surprised by the gesture.

Thora nibbled on the food as she spoke about her seemingly previous life. "The Norsk life is a hard one. We farm and fight, all the time."

"Fight with whom?" Halcyon asked. She cut more meat and placed it on another slice of bread.

"Amongst ourselves because our leaders oppose each other."

"Did you fight?"

Thora swallowed her mouthful first, then replied, "A little... for my husband's honor."

Halcyon paused and looked up from the food in her palm. "You are married, then?"

"Only for one year before our village was attacked by an enemy." Thora's old memories filtered back to her. "He was killed, and I became a slave."

Halcyon now understood Thora's path to Greece. "Do you have children?"

Thora shook her head and picked up a piece of lamb.

"Tell me more about your life there," Halcyon said.

Thora did so and continued conversing with her owner about the Norsk life. She was amazed that Halcyon asked so many questions. They had lost track of time until Cesare was closing the gate.

Cesare locked the gate, then came over to the pair. "It is getting late, ěra."

Halcyon eyed Cesare, who had been in her service for many years. She held favor for him, but as she turned her attention to Thora, she realized she had developed a larger favor for Thora.

"It is late." Thora stood after seconding Cesare.

Halcyon slotted her eyes at the pair. "As I recall, I am the head of this house."

Cesare bristled at those words, but he tensed further when Thora spoke back.

"Not until your shoulder is fully healed, ĕra." Thora ignored the minor irritation in Halcyon's features, waiting to be contested by Halcyon. After a beat, she smoothly said, "Until then, I believe you are outnumbered."

Cesare nervously shifted on his feet.

Halcyon stood up and looked directly at Thora. "Perhaps, more outwitted." She picked up the empty olive bowl. "I will only comply if this is refilled."

Thora took the bowl that glistened with honey. "I will bring it to your room."

Halcyon accepted the deal and went upstairs, her walk slow.

Cesare lowered his eyes to the bowl in Thora's hands. "She has never favored olives with honey in the past."

Thora lifted the bowl closer to her chest. She, too, thought it was quite strange.

"Do you think there is something wrong?" Cesare worried himself over his owner. "She is not herself."

Thora silently agreed with Cesare, but her concerns were on a different path from Cesare's own. She suspected their owner would be displeased if Cesare knew for certain that something was amiss about her. Thora brushed his concerns aside and said, "She is still healing."

Cesare nodded and quietly replied, "Both physical and mental."

Turning the bowl, Thora watched the honey move around the artistic decoration of a hoplite in the base. "*Já.*" She went to the kitchen.

Cesare sighed and collected a few dishes from the table. He followed Thora's cold trail to the kitchen, hoping Halcyon would return to normal.

⟨HA⅄TƐR TWƐL⅄Ɛ

Thora was startled awake by a scream, and she tossed the fur off her body, noticing that Glauce sat up too. Another scream told her it was their owner, so she hastily climbed to her feet. When Glauce started to rise, she said, "Stay here."

In a heartbeat, Thora was outside of her shared room and saw Cesare step out of his room to see what was wrong. "I will see to her."

Cesare nodded and returned to his room.

Another scream made Thora hasten to the thalamus. The soft candlelight helped her see Halcyon's distress in her sleep. Bending over the bed, Thora gently shook her owner.

"Wake up, ĕra!"

Halcyon thrashed a few times before Thora's voice cut through her dreamscape, eyes open and wild. Her right arm shot up, and her fingers wrapped around Thora's throat.

Thora grappled with her owner's muscular arm but fell to her knees. She gritted her teeth as her heart slammed against her chest. Suddenly, air rushed into her lungs when she was released from the death grip.

"Thora!" Halcyon growled, sitting up and touching Thora's shoulders. "You know not to touch me when I sleep." She checked over Thora, who was coughing hard.

Thora had once been instructed not to touch her owner while she slept, due to her training as a hoplite. Tonight she had been far too concerned and forgot the warning. "I have learned why now."

Halcyon had a worried look. "Sit." She inspected the marks on Thora's neck. She frowned, remembering Thora had healed from such markings from her husband.

"You were having a bad dream and stirred the entire house." Thora rubbed her neck.

"I know. You are safer to throw my helmet at me than touch me."

Thora huffed and dropped her hand from her neck, noticing her owner's playful smile. "I will do so next time." She then stood up. "I hope you sleep better than before." She started for the door until Halcyon's husky voice called to her.

"Sleep in my bed... tonight."

Thora had half turned to her owner, somewhat revealing her mild shock and open mouth.

"It is the least I can do after I strangled you." Halcyon patiently waited for a choice.

"And what if you strangle me again in our sleep?"

Halcyon tasted the humor in the words. "I will not."

After a heave breath, Thora considered the offer for a better night's sleep on a bed rather than on the floor, mostly accustom to the floor, but a soft bed was a wonderful prospect. Slowly she drifted to the empty side of the bed and was invited in when Halcyon pushed the fur aside for her. Noticing Halcyon's pleased smile, Thora said nothing and snuggled under the cool furs.

"Glauce will notice my absence."

Halcyon closed her eyes after she adjusted the fur. "Perhaps." She then whispered, "If so, then she will not speak about it."

Thora shut her eyes too and contently sighed, quickly drifting off after she relaxed beside her owner.

Halcyon eventually turned onto her right side and had quieter dreams instead of nightmares about war. By morning, she noticed that the bed was empty and suspected Thora was up before daybreak. After dressing in a yellow chiton,

Halcyon started for the courtyard until the constant nausea increased and forced her to hurry to the ouranē.

"Hades," Halcyon growled, hating mornings! Her weakened body brought her to her knees beside the damn ouranē. Halcyon tried to be quiet, but the sounds still alerted Thora. Sandals' soft hits across stone floor registered with her.

Thora was at her side and helped her sit up after the sickness, wiping her face clean. She remained knelt beside Halcyon and worriedly studied fatigued features.

Lifting her head off the wall, Halcyon rasped, "I am okay."

Thora placed her hand against Halcyon's good shoulder. "You are with child."

Halcyon stiffened and stared coldly at Thora.

"That is why King Leonidas sent you home." Thora placed the linen on the floor and looked at Halcyon's stomach. "I only realized yesterday why you have been so sick and craving strange things like olives with honey."

Halcyon's stare was still hard, and she breathed heavily, uncertain wha to say.

"I have not spoken about this to anybody." Thora sensed deep anger inside Halcyon. "You are unhappy about this." She shook her head and asked, "Why?"

"There is a great war burning for our freedom. And this thing has weakened me to the point I cannot wield my xiphos." Halcyon's voice trembled from her rage.

"It is a child!" Thora reached forward and placed her hand against Halcyon's stomach. "A gift from the gods."

"It is a curse that has taken me from my duties," Halcyon said, bitingly.

Thora shook her head. "There can be no hoplites without children. The gods could have ended your life at the tip of a sword, but they gave you a child and a future far beyond your own." She raised her hands and cupped flushed cheeks. "You are still a hoplite, and soon you will bear another. It is a blessing."

Halcyon lowered her head for a beat but refused her slave's words, needing the distance.

After a low huff, Thora stood and noticed Halcyon's weak motions. "I once dreamed about having a son or a daughter, but now—" Her eyes stung, but she withheld her tears. "Now I wish not to bring a child into slavery."

Halcyon closed her eyes just as a wave of dizziness hit her. "Thoraaa..."

Thora saw the unsteady motions and pulled Halcyon closer for support. "It will pass." She held onto Halcyon, who moaned from the spinning world.

Halcyon gripped the steady body. "I wish... for this to... cease." She leaned her head against Thora's shoulder.

"It will improve," Thora whispered then grinned. "It is only for nine months." She received a low grumble.

"I will place you in charge of the child," Halcyon said in warning.

Thora smiled at the threat. "I shall enjoy that." Her grin grew bigger still. "I will teach the child much about Norsk ways."

Groaning, Halcyon started straightening up, but she kept one hand on Thora. "The gods forbid that I have another Norsk likeminded person in my household."

Thora chuckled, then became serious. "Perhaps fresh air in the courtyard will help."

Halcyon conceded and exited the latrine. "I will go to the bouleuterion this morning." She descended the steps slowly. "You will join me."

"*Já.*" Thora followed down to the courtyard, then departed and mixed a mouth rinse in the kitchen.

Halcyon gratefully took the rinse and returned the small cup. Thora promised to bring her a morning meal shortly. After Thora left, Halcyon was greeted by Yarikh, and she invited him to join her for the meal.

Yarikh obliged, and together they dined over conversation. He finally had a chance to visit with Halcyon for the first time since her return from Thermopylae, many days ago. Occasionally, he caught himself staring at the scar across Halcyon's left eye. Many images ran through his mind of how Halcyon earned the wound. For an hour, he and Halcyon discussed Thora's advancements with Greek. He could tell that Halcyon was rather pleased with him, but he only had a little time left before he had to travel home.

Thora returned to the courtyard after she and Glauce ate a quick meal in the kitchen. She asked Glauce to clean up. Halcyon took the cue to leave for the bouleuterion. She bid Yarikh goodbye, then headed through the courtyard, out the gate, and onto the streets. Thora faithfully followed behind her to the agora.

Similar to yesterday, nearly every seat at the bouleuterion was occupied by citizens. The talks were renewed on how large an army to send against King Xerxes. By early afternoon, the decisions were declared and the army leaders given orders. Within days, the Spartan army would march north to face the Persian king and his large army.

Halcyon was relieved by the outcome because it meant her king's sacrifice was not in vain. She prayed his soul would make safe passage to Elysium. As people left the bouleuterion, she watched Gorgo speak with different councilmen. Halcyon suspected Gorgo expected her husband would return upon his shield any day now. Such truth even stung Halcyon, who now had a spouse going to the war. She decided it was best to visit Euclid before he started his march.

"Ěra?"

Halcyon broke from her thoughts and said, "Wait here." She left her seat, then went down the steps.

Thora curiously watched her owner and Gorgo interact and smile at each other. They seemed to be in an agreement about something. Moments later, Halcyon climbed the steps and ordered Thora to accompany her home.

Once they returned home, Halcyon mentioned, "Queen Gorgo will be joining me this evening."

Thora now understood what had passed between them at the bouleuterion.

"I plan to rest for a while so that I am... pleasant company."

Thora dipped her head. "I will wake you before she arrives."

Only nodding, Halcyon continued through the courtyard and went up to the second level, her steps softly fading away.

However, Thora remained beside the pool and considered tonight's guest. She had a thin frown and a worried expression, but she went about her duties. She made sure to inform Glauce and Cesare of Halcyon's guest. They had to ensure the villa was presentable, especially because it was Queen Gorgo.

When the sun hung in the western sky, Thora broke away from her duties, stirred her owner awake, and checked over the improving wounds. She asked Halcyon if she needed help preparing for tonight but was told to finish in the kitchen. Shortly after, Halcyon went downstairs into the andron and was pleased that everything was set up correctly for her guest. She then took a seat with a tablet in the courtyard until Gorgo's arrival.

At the open gate, Gorgo called for attention and smiled at Halcyon crossing the courtyard. After a warm exchange, they sat together by the fountain's bench.

Halcyon sat closely beside the beautiful queen. "Thank you for joining me this evening."

Gorgo smiled and bowed her head. "I was greatly pleased by your invitation." She let her smile slip and softly said, "I have been concerned about your health." In her letter from Leonidas, her husband explained that he had returned Halcyon to Sparta because of pregnancy. So far, she had kept the information close to her chest, but she thought it necessary to be made public to save face for the Iron Edge.

Halcyon composed her words carefully, but she held her silence as Thora arrived with two skyphoi. Glauce followed out with the wine oinochoe and filled the two skyphoi. She quietly returned to the kitchen. Thora was about to follow until Halcyon touched her arm.

"Queen Gorgo and I will be in the andron."

Thora merely moved her head in understanding and departed from the courtyard.

Gorgo's eyes followed the unusual, beautiful slave. "She is rather quiet."

Halcyon stood up and led the way to the andron, Gorgo's observation churning in her mind. It was rather strange for Thora to be reserved, even around guests. She made no comment, though, and instead took a seat.

Gorgo was pleased to stretch out on a kline and took in the room's fine décor. She pondered what may have come from Halcyon's family or Euclid's own. She knew this to be the andron, reserved only for men. However, it was clear that Halcyon bore the power.

"Your sculptures are magnificent."

Following her guest's gaze, Halcyon looked at the bronze sculpture of Athena that she had received the sculpture from her father after she competed in the Heraea Games. It was also her most favorite in the room.

"Who did your painting of Aphrodite?" Gorgo pointed with her skyphos, index finger stretched out toward the opposite wall.

Halcyon trailed her eyes over to the painted wall on her right. A thin smile graced her lips, and she replied, "An artist from Athens named Olus."

"It is beautiful." Gorgo loved how Aphrodite stretched out upon a sandy beach and gazed upon the room as if it were the ocean. Her toga was drawn back to reveal her right breast. Her green eyes bore the seas in them.

"Thank you," Halcyon softly replied.

Gorgo shifted her attention to Halcyon. "You did not answer my earlier question."

Halcyon released a soft sigh. "My health has improved greatly."

"Almost fully healed?" Gorgo checked, pulling her legs and feet up onto the kline. She hardly expected Halcyon to reveal the pregnancy, at least not yet.

"Yes."

Letting go of the discussion, Gorgo understood that Halcyon could be both a private and strong-willed person. She instead shifted the conversation to the recent politics, curious to learn Halcyon's opinion about Sparta sending the army to battle. Their conversation was interrupted by the arrival of the meal.

Halcyon curiously studied Thora, who moved carefully with the plates of food. She noted Glauce handled serving Gorgo, who was ignored by Thora. Halcyon tucked her observations away and renewed the earlier conversation.

Thora finished serving and refilled Halcyon's skyphos. She then went to the andron's doorway and waited for Glauce. In those few moments, she watched how Halcyon focused intently on Gorgo. Thora clenched the oinochoe tighter. A harsh burn started low in her chest, but she clenched down on it.

Glauce finished tending to Gorgo and left with Thora. She noticed the tension lines on Thora's face. "What concerns you?"

Thora's cheeks flushed, and she sighed before calmly saying, "All is well." She and Glauce entered the kitchen to put together a quick sweet dish to follow the main meal.

Gorgo and Halcyon continued conversing well after sunset. Glauce returned with the sweet dish and lit more candles in the room. She refilled the women's cups, then left them alone.

Halcyon was uncertain about Thora's lack of appearance and would question her later. She remained focused on Gorgo, who greatly intrigued her. She had always admired Gorgo's strength, especially when it came to politics. Halcyon had steered away from the politics simply because a hoplite's lifestyle was simple and logical. She loved it. But Gorgo's will to hold power in the political games was an amazement.

Eventually, Halcyon walked Gorgo to the gate and called for Cesare to accompany them back to Gorgo's home. Together, they crossed through the city until they came to a large home, and a helot opened the gate.

"Thank you for tonight," Gorgo said.

Halcyon offered a smile. "I enjoyed your company."

Gorgo was happy to spend time with Halcyon. She was trying to remain busy before she surely received her husband's body upon his shield. She ignored what was in her future, and Halcyon was an excellent distraction.

"Perhaps tomorrow evening you can join me again."

Gorgo's eyes brightened at the prospect. "At the same time?"

"If you wish." Halcyon bowed her head in respect.

Gorgo raised her hand and gently brushed her fingertips over Halcyon's jaw line. "I will see you then."

"Goodnight, my queen." Halcyon straightened up and stole a last glance at the beautiful queen. She quietly left with Cesare on her heels.

Once back at home, Halcyon found that the kitchen was clean and also dim. She went upstairs and noted that both female slaves were in their shared room. Halcyon moved away from the slaves' room and silently went to the thalamus. She had plans to see Euclid the next day before he left for war. However, early in the morning, she would corner Thora and find out what was wrong. As she prepared for bed, Halcyon replayed her evening with Gorgo and looked forward to her company tomorrow.

ᑕHAPTΣR THIRTΣΣN

After a entering the bathing room, Glauce bowed to her owner, then carried clean clothes and checked that a dry linen was ready too.

"Glauce?" Halcyon was comfortable in the bathing pool. "Where is Thora?"

"She is with Yarikh this morning," Glauce replied. She caught Halcyon's unreadable emotion and shifted on her feet. "Is there anything else you need, ěra?"

Halcyon waved off Glauce, who silently took her exit from the room. She pushed aside her concerns and decided that she was too sensitive to Thora. Today would be spent with Euclid before he left for war, then Gorgo would visit for an evening meal together.

The morning had begun similarly to others, and Halcyon hated the morning sickness. However, Thora had not come to her aid, and she waited alone as the sickness calmed down. This morning's bath had helped soothe away the aches of early pregnancy, but it was only temporary.

After preparing for her day, Halcyon went to the kitchen in hopes to inform Thora about tonight's guest. She frowned at Glauce by the oven. Glauce detected the annoyance and nervously moved about the kitchen.

"Where is Thora?" Halcyon asked for the second time today.

"At the agora, ěra."

Halcyon softly sighed and gave a faint nod. "Inform her that Queen Gorgo will be here this evening." She would speak to Thora later.

"Yes, of course." Glauce was beside the large metal pot that hung over an open fire. She stirred the contents in it. Her stomach remained knotted from the tension. She and Halcyon had yet to fully reconcile from the fight about the kitchen fire.

Halcyon slipped out of the room and sought out Cesare. Once she located him, she left her villa with Cesare in tow. Together, they went to Euclid's assigned barracks. Halcyon visited with him for some time, and they discussed many things about their war with King Xerxes. By midday, Halcyon took her leave and wished Euclid safety in battle. She hoped to see him again, but they kissed for perhaps the last time.

Halcyon never revealed her pregnancy to Euclid.

* * *

In the afternoon, Halcyon spent time at the bouleuterion and listened to the latest politics, secretly hoping to see Gorgo, who was absent. Eventually, Halcyon left the building and met Cesare outside on the street. Their walk home was long, due to the marching hoplites leaving the city. Halcyon recognized several faces under the helmets, and she wished her brothers well. She would pray to Ares and Athena for them.

At home, the kitchen was busy with Thora and Glauce's preparations for an evening meal. Gorgo arrived an hour after Halcyon returned home. It was early, and the two freewomen decided to sit in the courtyard while the sunlight still allowed it. They talked happily, drank wine, and shared olives. Only once had Thora appeared to refill their wine but only because Glauce was too busy preparing the meal. Before the meal was ready, Halcyon directed Gorgo into the andron where they would be more comfortable.

Cesare finished lighting the candles in the andron. He gazed over at Glauce and Thora when they came through the open doors. He noted their full hands, so he hastily helped them distribute the dishes. Glauce gave Cesare an appreciative smile. She and Thora quietly left together.

Cesare took a step back, toward the door. "Anything else, ĕra?"

Halcyon put a handful of grapes into her palm. "No, but thank you, Cesare."

Gorgo was enjoying the fish on her plate. "You treat your slaves well."

Tilting her head, Halcyon waited to see if Gorgo would say anything else.

Since last night, Gorgo had taken stock of the well-dressed and groomed slaves in Halcyon's house. The slaves also looked exceptionally healthy. Today she had even given it thought about the one barbarian slave's skill with their native Greek tongue.

"How did your slave..." Gorgo mentally searched for the slave's name.

Instantly, Halcyon knew which slave sparked the Gorgo's interest. "Thora," she supplied.

Gorgo nodded and lowered the plate to the small table between them. "How did Thora learn Greek?"

Halcyon had finished her grapes and took the second plate of herbed fish. "Perhaps from her previous owner."

Gorgo considered it then said, "She is bright for a barbar."

Halcyon bit the inside of her mouth to contain her harsh retort. She had automatically taken offense to her favorite slave, Thora, being called a barbarian. In that instant, Halcyon realized how greatly her emotions toward Thora had changed over the months. She shifted uncomfortably on the kline, then peered down at the partially eaten fish.

"I wish I had such intelligent slaves." Gorgo popped a torn piece of bread into her mouth. "Perhaps I will have you select my next one."

Halcyon peered up, green eyes bright. "Perhaps."

Gorgo grinned and ate the last morsel of bread. "I have enjoyed these last two evenings with you, Halcyon."

After a swallow, Halcyon flashed a slight smile. "I, too." She crossed her legs. "I have hoped to distract you from thoughts of your husband."

Gorgo grew solemn at the mention of Leonidas. "I..." She cleared her throat, but her voice was weak. "I expect his shield any day."

Halcyon thought of Euclid, who was possibly marching to his own death. "I am sorry, my queen."

Gorgo had picked up her wine, but she stretched out her other hand and rested it on Halcyon's covered knee. "We both understand what our husbands must do, just as we must do for Sparta." She pulled her hand away. "You understand better than any."

Halcyon still felt the warmth against her skin from Gorgo's tender touch. She wanted to push the sensation away but was drawn deeper into it when she met Gorgo's honey-brown gaze. She parted her lips, but her words failed her.

Thora and Glauce quietly entered the room and refilled the wine. They collected two empty plates that had the fish.

Halcyon had a chance to compose herself, but her attention remained on Gorgo, who gave her a smile. Halcyon was warmed by the affection and nearly lost her thoughts again.

"Thank you." Gorgo smiled at Glauce, who took her plate.

Halcyon blinked out of her daydream. She glanced over at the two slaves, who slipped out of the andron. For a moment, a frown played on her lips.

"Halcyon?" Shortly dark green eyes settled on Gorgo. She then asked, "Tell me about your upbringing to become a hoplite." She had heard many stories among different circles. Tonight was her chance to learn it directly from Halcyon.

There was no other female hoplite, and Gorgo doubted there would ever be another.

A few hours later, Glauce returned to perform her checks. She deposited bowls of fruit and olives on the table between the pair. She then dismissed herself but felt her owner's eyes on her.

"You are distracted, Halcyon." Gorgo had a handful of olives. She curiously studied Halcyon's troubled profile. "What worries you?"

Halcyon bottled her emotions that were weakening her lately, much like the pregnancy. She had grown too sensitive, especially toward Thora. Why it bothered her that Thora avoided her should hold no weight. Yet Halcyon continued expecting Thora to attend to her, not Glauce.

"I have not been myself of late," Halcyon told.

Gorgo weighed such truth as she chewed on an olive. She nodded and sat up from her reclined position. "You have recently returned from battle. You are still healing from wounds." She brushed her hands clean of the olives' salt. "Now your husband has been sent to war."

Halcyon's jaw flexed with tension. Her wild emotions had taken on too much life. She attributed it to her pregnancy and subconsciously slid her hand over her belly.

"And he may return on his shield," Gorgo said sadly. She looked from the table to the silent woman on the other kline. She noticed Halcyon's eyes were closed and slowly her gaze traveled down to the hand that cupped Halcyon's stomach. Gorgo had a slight smile at the secret.

Halcyon shifted on the kline and said, "Perhaps you are correct." She straightened more. "I hardly feel well now." Her own words seemed to bring on the nausea.

Gorgo indeed noticed the pale hue across Halcyon's face. She rose and went to Halcyon's aid. "Let me help you." She gathered Halcyon's free hand into her own. "Perhaps it would be best if you rested now." She read the struggle within Halcyon. "We can meet again."

"I am afraid I have become a bore." Halcyon received a warm smile for the jest.

"Hardly." Gorgo stood. "Come now." She wished for Halcyon to rest and assisted Halcyon to her feet. "I enjoyed my evening with you."

"As I." Halcyon was guided out of the andron and into the dark courtyard.

Gorgo squeezed Halcyon's callused hand before she let go. From the corner of her eye, she saw the male slave, Cesare, enter the courtyard from the kitchen. She was grateful when he gave pause beside the pool.

"I hope to regain my strength soon."

Gorgo smiled, broadly. "I doubt anytime soon, Halcyon." She pressed a hand against the other woman's belly. "Pregnancy is tiring." She was startled by the sudden alarm on Halcyon's face. She quickly removed her touch from Halcyon's stomach and captured a hand. "I have been with child once. I know the signs." She then softly told, "Besides, your king told me why you returned."

Halcyon was stiff and uneasy, hating her pregnancy was becoming obvious to people. She needed to hide her body's weak state.

"I understand why my husband sent you home." Gorgo tightened her grip on Halcyon's hand. "He was wise to do so."

Cesare distantly heard the women's voices, but they were muffled. He took a seat on the corner of the pool's wall. He heard a soft movement behind him, and he looked back at the kitchen's entrance. He noted Thora and Glauce, but he stiffened at Thora's fierce attention on their owner. Slowly, Cesare turned his head back toward his owner and Gorgo. Much to his surprise, Halcyon was being kissed by Gorgo.

Halcyon felt her bottom lip pull with Gorgo's teeth before it was released, which ended their too brief kiss. If she had been alarmed earlier, she was far more distraught now.

Gorgo withdrew her hand from Halcyon's wavy tendrils of soft hair. She brushed her fingertips across Halcyon's palm as they released hands. "You must consider telling the reason for your return." She left Halcyon with heavy thoughts as she stepped away. "Thank you for tonight."

Halcyon was at a loss. She loathed her pregnancy, but Gorgo was clearly concerned with her honor as a hoplite. She stood rooted in the courtyard and stared at the departing queen. She then sensed Cesare at her side.

"I will walk her home, ĕra."

Halcyon dipped her head in agreement. She was pleased by Cesare's care. But once alone in the courtyard, she dragged her fingers through her hair and blew out a heavy sigh. "Gods!" she whispered. Her mind was muddled by tonight's unforeseen events.

Finally, Halcyon gathered her messy pieces and turned toward the kitchen. She crossed the courtyard but slowed once she realized there was no light from the kitchen. She remained poised in the dark entranceway. She was disjointed for a heartbeat again and shook off the obvious fact that Thora was evading her. She pushed away from the entrance and went up the stairs.

Inside the kitchen, Thora remained silent even though she heard footsteps grow distant. She continued pressing her back into the cool stone of the kitchen's wall, just beside the entrance to the courtyard. She leaned her head against the wall and closed her eyes. Again and again, her mind repeated the kiss between her owner and Gorgo.

Sometime ago, Thora had been rid of Selene, who held contempt for Thora and even Halcyon. After being subjected to Selene, Thora thought Halcyon would be content with solitude for a time. But now it was Gorgo, who was more than a freewoman and more than just a queen. Gorgo was a woman of generosity and heart, yet still strong. And she was a woman who now broke Thora's heart. All she believed she and Halcyon had built between them would bend and fracture in days. Thora would relearn her place in life.

Several prayers passed her lips and went to her Norsk gods. She pleaded for them to hear her. She wished for her Norsk homelands again. Her emotions clawed at a past that was lost in the chains of slavery by a woman who could walk among the gods. Thora's life belonged to iron and silence, to transparency and loneliness. No longer could her gods reach her and pluck her out of this life. She bowed her head to it.

Eventually, Thora gathered the remainder of her strength and carried herself upstairs. She silently slipped into her shared quarters and crumbled to her furs. Her ugly dreams taunted her until daylight.

* * *

The next day, Thora slipped into her meaningless duties like any slave in a Greek house. Glauce and Cesare helped her without question. When Thora heard the dry heaves from upstairs, she strangled down her sympathy and continued her tasks. Glauce was beside the oven, and their owner's distress made her look to Thora. She clearly saw the restraint written on Thora's features. She parted her lips, prepared to speak dangerous words. She lost her courage and looked back at the oven.

Thora gripped the knife harder each time another one of Halcyon's heaves echoed down the stairs. She blew out a breath when she heard only the crackle from the oven's fire. She refocused on the vegetable in her right hand and the knife in her left. She continued slicing.

"I must go to the agora," Thora said suddenly.

Glauce turned her head toward Thora. "I will accompany you."

Thora continued chopping the carrots. "Ĕra will need your help." She looked at Glauce. "Not I."

Shortly, Thora left the home from the courtyard. She had a brief sense of relief, now that she was free of the house. Pieces of her mind imagined going past the agora, down the road, and leaving it all.

Upon her return back home, Thora was startled by Gorgo's presence in the courtyard. She gathered her wits by stealing a quiet moment to relock the front gate. She slowly turned with a full sack in her hand.

"Hello, Thora." Gorgo was seated on a bench beside the pool. She was alone, for now. She rose as Thora approached her, but she was still short under the slave's height. She wondered how Halcyon had control over a slave with such stature.

Thora assessed Gorgo, before she finally bowed her head. "Can I assist you with anything?"

Gorgo hummed at the weak request. "I only wait for your ĕra."

Thora imagined Halcyon would join Gorgo shortly.

Sensing Thora's disapproval, Gorgo curiously mentioned, "She was worn last night." She wondered if her attempt would reach past Thora's protective stance, wondering why she cared about Thora's acceptance.

Thora dipped her head then retreated toward the kitchen but heard Gorgo's next remark.

"I care for her well-being."

Hesitating, Thora gazed over her shoulder, remained silent, and vanished into the kitchen. Eventually, voices from the courtyard reached her ears, prompting Thora to work faster so her mind was busy.

"Thora?" Cesare entered the kitchen. "We must organize wine and food for ĕra and the queen."

"Yes." Thora was already preparing food. She looked over to Cesare in the entranceway. "Glauce?"

Cesare nodded and hurried off to locate Glauce. He returned with her, then went to check on his owner.

Glauce prepared what food Thora had put together, and they went into the courtyard with the filled dishes in their hands and on their arms. Cesare noted there was no wine, so he hurried into the kitchen. Surely, Halcyon was parched after today's practice on the field.

Thora and Glauce put the plates around the table between the two freewomen. Thora placed one clean dish in front of Gorgo, then moved the second one in front of Halcyon. She only made it one step before Halcyon hooked her wrist. Gradually, her blue eyes locked with dark green ones. Halcyon exchanged a silent battle of wills with Thora.

"Halcyon," Gorgo said for the third time. She was relieved when green eyes cut to her. "Tell me about your training today."

Halcyon felt Thora break free, and she allowed it, more interested in Gorgo. She responded to Gorgo's request, and her hands moved with her explanation about her practice today. She had hardly expected training to be cut short by Gorgo's unexpected arrival. But, it pleased her nonetheless.

Slowly, Halcyon's annoyance with Thora receded under Gorgo's visit. She and Gorgo shared a few laughs and plenty of smiles. When the sunlight dimmed in the courtyard, Halcyon suggested they retire to the andron. Together, she and Gorgo stood up from their seats and went to the sealed door of the andron, guiding them into it. After lighting the candles, Halcyon shared a kline with Gorgo. There was hardly any space between them as they sat beside each other, hand in hand.

Thora had slipped into the room with two filled skyphoi. She slowed beside the table and stared coldly at Gorgo's lips pressed against Halcyon's own. She put the skyphoi on the table, loudly. Halcyon broke from the kiss and turned her annoyed features on Thora.

Gorgo shifted her free hand onto her lower stomach, startled by Thora's subtle defiance. She met the icy glare directed at her and Halcyon. She felt the fire building in Halcyon. Thora straightened up and wordlessly left the andron.

Gorgo released a shaky breath. She nearly spoke, but Halcyon rose from the kline. "Halcyon?"

"I will return," Halcyon said, vanishing from the andron. Her tide of anger carried her to the other side of the house and into the kitchen. Her presence stifled the kitchen, more than any heat or smoke from the oven.

Glauce was cleaning dishes but tensed at the fiery look. She quickly realized that all of Halcyon's ire was locked on Thora, who stood behind the square island with a knife.

"Leave us, Glauce."

As soft footsteps faded, Thora flexed her fingers on the knife's handle. She willed herself to let it go, then lifted her head until she met dark features.

"You insult me," Halcyon growled, stomping up to the wooden block that separated them.

Thora swallowed her emotions, except for her ferocity. Her steely blue eyes matched Halcyon's green. "How can slave insult owner?"

Halcyon pressed her hands flat against the island and leaned closer. "By insulting the owner's guest." She tilted her head. "Who is more than just a guest — she is the queen." She immediately noticed a bitter spark in Thora's eyes. "Why do you insult me?" She straightened up. "I thought we had moved forward."

"Forward impossible. There is no forward for slaves." Thora started around the tall block, features worn from the growing fight.

Halcyon took a sidestep and blocked Thora's retreat. From their close proximity, she sighed at the distress in Thora's fiery eyes. She remembered the one and only time when Thora had such enraged emotions. But further behind it was a wall of bitterness that had been built over time.

Thora lifted her chin, but she held her spot. She towered over her owner, and yet her owner's strength was imposing. "Flog me. Punish me."

Halcyon's lips curled into a sneer. "I seem to have already done that — with Gorgo." She hit a nerve and saw Thora flinch under the icy truth. Her glare softened under the obvious pain that had been buried in Thora. Halcyon's angry fog cleared with the revelation, and she said, "Speak the truth to me."

Thora controlled her body's weakness, but her voice trembled when she moved her lips. "I carried a blade before this life." She lifted her left hand and studied her palm, which was clean, but she still saw the blood. "I protected what was mine." She looked at Halcyon again. "Until it was taken, killed, and I was brought here." She stepped closer to Halcyon and whispered, "Now nothing is mine." She nearly reached for Halcyon. "Not even my ĕra." This time, she moved past Halcyon.

"That is because you are mine." Halcyon turned her head sidelong and saw Thora pause in the entranceway. Thora turned and studied Halcyon's rigid back.

"I plucked you out of that slaver's centaur feces." Halcyon neared Thora again.

"Why?"

Halcyon tilted her head. "Your hair is the sun." She ruefully smiled. "Your eyes are the sky." Her smile shifted into a grin. "You stand taller than our gods." She watched Thora's weak headshake. "And your defiance warms me." She huffed and coolly said, "You deserved better than to become a helot."

Thora gave a low sigh, then drifted toward the courtyard, needing the space. "I will ask Glauce to attend to you and Queen Gorgo." She was hardly fit to handle them. "Have a pleasant night, ĕra." She was resigned in her words.

"Thora." Halcyon took in Thora's exhausted posture and worn features, knowing there was no reason to have Thora attend to her and Gorgo tonight. "It is not Queen Gorgo whom I wish to warm my bed." Halcyon allowed the rest to remain unspoken as she broke away and returned to the andron.

Thora closed her eyes and whispered, "I wish the same."

⟨HΛᗺƬƐR FϘURƬƐᑎ

Leather sandals smacked against wooden flooring at an alarming pace. Glauce called again for her owner while she ran to the thalamus. In her fisted hand, shredded ends of cloth waved in the warm morning air. Glauce pushed into her owner's room, without dignity or care. The slight candlelight and sun's dawning barely showed her flushed features.

"Ěra!"

Halcyon had arisen only moments ago when her morning sickness forced her. She peered across her shoulder at the frantic slave. "What is it?"

Glauce ignored the impatience and hastily handed over a scrap of cloth, which had strange letters written on it. She shook her head and frantically said, "She is gone, ěra."

Halcyon reread the bold word that was scratched into the material. Each letter had foreign arms and legs, but to her Norsk slave, it was familiar.

"She left last night... while we slept." Glauce knotted and unknotted her fingers several times. "I only found this where her roll should be."

Halcyon barely registered the ramble. She heard enough to assume that Thora had probably taken some provisions. She curled her hand around the cloth and whispered, "You may go."

Glauce parted her lips but held her silence. She bowed her head and took a step back. She turned and almost passed the thalamus's entrance until her owner's voice gave her pause.

"Send for Yarikh." Halcyon briefly listened to the departure but returned her focus to the scrap in her hand. Again, the foreign word spoke to her, yet its translation was lost on Halcyon. What did transfer into Halcyon was the raw power in each stroke of the letters. She felt the sorrow and brokenness when Thora dragged the black chalk across the linen. Yarikh's arrival broke her thoughts.

"Can you read this?" Halcyon handed the cloth to him.

Yarikh studied the strange letters that were from a language unknown to him. He had learned tidbits of Thora's spoken language, but the written one was a mystery. When he turned over the cloth, he stared oddly at what appeared to be one word. "I am unsure what it says on one side."

Halcyon was studying Yarikh. She seemed patient, but anxiety was building under her skin. The scrap of cloth was her only clue to Thora's very existence.

"But," Yarikh said, "I believe this is an apology." He displayed the single word on the stained side of the cloth. "Fyrirgef."

Halcyon received the cloth and stared at the Norsk word. She turned it over and wished she could read what Thora had scratched on the other side. It was a full sentence in smaller print compared to the apology. Halcyon closed her eyes briefly before she met Yarikh's curious gaze.

"Has something-"

"You leave in the next day?" Halcyon asked.

Yarikh hesitated at the change, but he nodded after a moment. "I am to leave tomorrow."

Halcyon rose up and said, "That is all, Yarikh." She watched him turn. "Thank you."

Yarikh held the appreciation close while he walked out of the room. But his sandals suddenly weighed heavy as iron. He faltered in the doorway then peered back. "Halcyon..."

Halcyon gazed over her shoulder toward him. Even from a distance, she saw his distress and struggle to speak up.

Yarikh softly cleared his throat. "Early on in our reading lessons, I showed Thora how to read maps." He faltered briefly when Halcyon narrowed her eyes. "She asked if I had other maps, larger ones. I only had one other that I brought with me from Rome." He laced his hands in front of himself, in hopes it would calm the ball of guilt in his lower belly. "It showed the routes in Gaul that Roman merchants travel for trade."

Halcyon slightly lifted her chin but tamped down on the sudden fire in her chest at Yarikh's mistake. He could not have known Thora's plans, she told herself.

"Yesterday I began to pack, and I noticed the map was gone." Yarikh's eyes fluttered a few times before he insisted, "I intended to ask her of it before I left."

Halcyon inhaled deeply and turned her head away. She realized she had balled her hands in her lap. "That is all, Yarikh." She willed him to leave and took another long breath as Yarikh's steps faded in the distance.

After a moment, Halcyon rose onto her unsteady feet. She became breathless and shaky in a few heartbeats. She hardened her resolve because she still had a walk to the latrine. Similar to previous mornings, she knelt before the ouranē and allowed the few contents to leave her stomach. She prayed to the gods that the sickness would soon leave her. It would be many months before she was truly well again. With bitterness, Halcyon left the latrine and nearly collided with Cesare.

"Ěra," Cesare said breathlessly, yet frantic lines were in his features. "Thora is gone."

"Yes, I am aware." Halcyon stepped around Cesare and slowly returned to the thalamus. "Ready two horses." She paused beside the entrance to the room. "Then come find me."

Cesare remained still and bowed his head after he decided it was better to follow orders than ask questions. He hurried off with a soft mutter.

Halcyon reentered her room and slowly moved about it. Every step and motion through the room gave her a chance to think more about Thora. From the first day, Halcyon had been drawn to Thora's spirit and loved the challenge. There was a renewed life in her home upon Thora's arrival. Now Halcyon felt the heaviness in the house.

"Ĕra." Cesare's presence disturbed his owner's thoughts. He stood in the doorway and appeared calmer, besides the few tells of stress marring his features.

Halcyon stood with her back to Cesare and continued closing the rucksack, then picked up the sheathed xiphos and a dagger.

"The horses are ready." Cesare had his hands behind his back with his fingers knotted together.

"Pack your things, Cesare." Halcyon fastened the sword to her side. "And meet me at the stable."

Cesare stared at the bronze helmet seated next to the rucksack on the foot of the bed. He licked his lips and bowed his head. "Yes, ĕra." He quietly left again.

Halcyon took a deep breath and ignored the strain the bronze armor made upon her body. She was a highly regarded hoplite among her people. From birth, she was trained to live beyond her body's limitations. With a straighter back, Halcyon picked up the rucksack, helmet, and weapon. She left the thalamus.

Down in the courtyard, Glauce waited for her but soon hurried off to the kitchen after Halcyon's orders. Halcyon left the house and went to the stable. She was welcomed by several horse whinnies. The musky, leathery air settled comfortably in Halcyon's chest. As she neared Cheimon's stall, she felt a thread of clarity come over her. She was working out a plan to find Thora.

Cheimon huffed warmly at her owner, knowing a ride was ahead of them. She tossed her head as Halcyon came into the stall. Cesare had already tacked her, and Cheimon impatiently stomped the solid ground with her hoof.

Halcyon had a thin smile. She and Cheimon shared a special bond since their first meeting. She considered their bond while she set the rucksack on the ground. For a moment, she took the time to hook her sword into place.

Cheimon pounded her hoof a few times. She was only happy when her owner took the reins. Halcyon had put on the rucksack but still carried the helmet in her left hand. She pushed open the stall door and guided her horse out of the stable. Cesare nearly collided with Halcyon, but he darted to the side and bowed to her.

"Get your horse and hurry."

Cesare was about to rush off, but he noted Glauce running to them. He took wide steps and accepted the two bags of supplies that Glauce had prepared for them. He would put the items into his own rucksack.

"Hurry, Cesare."

Cesare vanished into the stable, shortly returning with a horse.

Halcyon was atop of her horse and slid on the helmet, seeming to become taller from the horsehair plume. She watched Cesare mount the horse. She grunted at his obvious trouble. "Can you no longer ride?" Many years ago, she had taught him to ride because she preferred his quiet company at times.

Cesare grumbled but became comfortable in the saddle. He silently cursed his aged body, but he would accompany his owner even if it caused aches in his joints. "I am old, ĕra, but not dead."

Under the shiny but scarred helmet, Halcyon's smile revealed itself. "Let us go, then." She tugged on the left rein and started the journey. Beyond her villa, she and Cesare rode through the streets of Sparta and steered around the carts or people. Once beyond the city, the worn road eventually was swallowed by the beautiful landscape.

Halcyon had long ago retained a mental map of the region after many marches to Corinth and Athens. If she and Cesare were to locate Thora, then their last chance was at the Diolkos along the Isthmus of Corinth. There were only a few spots that allowed traffic to cross the portage road along the isthmus. However, it would take them four and half days to ride to Corinth. Her hope was to catch up to Thora before the portage road, if they were fortunate to be following her trail. Halcyon knew Thora was highly intelligent and would steer away from villages where she could be captured for slavery, again. Thora's very appearance and stature made her stand out like the Minotaur.

At a fast pace, Halcyon traveled northeast as Apollo rode across the sky and shined light on the beautiful lands. Cesare faithfully rode behind his owner and kept a careful eye out for trouble. By Halcyon's overly stiff posture, he knew she was suffering, but he remained silent about it. They took several breaks, including near a stream for the horses to forage it.

When the sun hung low in the sky, Cesare pressed his horse to catch up. He had done his best to withhold his concerns about Halcyon's struggle, but it was now late afternoon. He believed it was best if they found a safe location for the night and rested, especially for Halcyon. However, it would be in poor taste to point out Halcyon's weakness. Cesare purposefully slumped forward against the horse, as if quite stricken.

"Ĕra."

Halcyon's attention was lost among the sea of hills that formed the peninsula. She broke away from her visual survey and silently questioned Cesare.

"It is late," Cesare said gently, "and these old bones of mine..."

Pursing her lips, Halcyon had been so occupied with her thoughts that she had missed Cesare's weariness, but she could hardly deny him or even herself. After a sharp nod, she smiled and said, "Not much farther."

Cesare was soon rewarded with a welcoming stream beyond a line of pistachio trees. With cautious movements, he dismounted from the horse and happily sighed to be finished riding for the day. After a glance to the west, he suspected they had less than two hours to organize the campsite. He took it upon himself to gather the firewood for the evening so that his owner could care for the horses.

Well before sunset, Halcyon and her slave were comfortably seated beside a fire. Few words passed between them as they shared a meal of dried meat, nuts, and uncooked vegetables. The fire was just enough to keep them warm, but it would be a cool night. Long ago, Halcyon was trained to snuff out campfires during the night. An unlit campsite attracted few to no bandits, along with chilly air.

Cesare wished Halcyon goodnight, then retired to his furs. He kept his back to the dying campfire and only heard Halcyon move a bit later. Eventually, the cool air nipped at his face, and he hid deeper into the furs.

Halcyon remained beside the campfire. She was wrapped in a fur that blocked out the evening chill. She watched the gentle dance of colors from the sunset. It was slow and yet so sudden to the end of a difficult day. Somewhere across the Grecian lands, her Norsk slave basked in the same sunset.

Thora had been named after the rumble that followed a spring storm. Indeed, Thora had swept across Halcyon's heart and struck a chord deep inside. Somehow, Halcyon found herself chasing the distant rumble, as if she were capable of touching the sky. As if Thora walked among the clouds. Halcyon vowed she would bring Thora back down.

Eventually, exhaustion claimed Halcyon. She only stirred a few times throughout the night, mainly to relieve herself. The morning birds woke her to the new day, and she found the campfire lit back to life. Halcyon was grateful for the warmth and reclaimed her seat by the fire.

Cesare busied with making a light breakfast for them. He was hardly a cook, but he could make do so that their bellies were full for the morning. Just as he nearly had the food ready, he watched Halcyon leave camp. Distantly, sounds of Halcyon's morning sickness drifted back to him. Cesare had yet to question Halcyon, but he knew the truth. It was the only truth that would cause King Leonidas to send home a prized hoplite with such prowess.

The morning meal passed in silence and then the pair broke camp at a steady pace. The horses were tacked quickly and soon the journey continued north, toward the Isthmus of Corinth. The hours burned into the next one until the beautiful mountains of Mainalo rose up in a soft green wave. Nestled below the mountain range was the busy city Mantineia. It was also Halcyon's navigational aid. From here, they would turn northeast toward the isthmus.

For a reward, Halcyon took a break in the city. They walked their horses to the agora and hitched them near a stable, then sought out supplies for their continued journey. Halcyon spent far too much time bartering over food. Mantineia was known for its wine and honey mead, but she steered away from it. It was hardly lost on her that Cesare had packed them water skins only. He knew about her pregnancy.

By late afternoon, they departed the busy town and continued northeast. The sun's afternoon heat warmed against their backs during the ride. Every hilltop and each valley rolled endlessly in a tide of terrain. The journey to the isthmus seemed mythical in size, but Halcyon knew it well from her time in the military. From Mantineia, Halcyon hoped to arrive at the isthmus in two to three days. If their timing was right and the Fates willed it, they would arrive before Thora and be able to halt her. They were perhaps already ahead of her, thanks to the horses.

Their chosen route was the only one off the peninsula, other than traveling by ship. Most likely ship passage was impossible for a tall, fair-haired, moneyless slave like Thora. Halcyon still wondered how she expected to escape back north. Thora was a shiny gold piece among the dark Greeks.

Cesare traded few words with his owner. At dinner, he noticed Halcyon was more sluggish than last night. Her pregnancy and the fast-paced travel were taxing, but there was little he could do to halt her. He had lost count of how many years he had been in Halcyon's grace, but it was long before Euclid. Halcyon had been merely a girl when Cesare was first purchased as part of the household. Now that brazen, chatty girl had transformed into a bronze, silent hoplite, yet still ever passionate.

After sunset, the campfire burned for longer than it had last night. Halcyon could barely find the strength to smother it. Its warmth eased her worries for her runaway slave. Tomorrow's first light would come soon, so she crumbled under the furs for the night. The heavy armor rested nearby with the sword propped up against the battle-worn helmet.

Cesare rested only shortly after Halcyon, who slept as heavily as him. The night's soft, cool air brushed his face, only a distant noise stirring him from a dream. He peeked out from beyond the furs and listened again for what had caught his ear. He may have only dreamed it, or it could have been an animal. Halcyon's continued sleep lulled him back to his dreamscape.

From under a pistachio tree, a leather-clad man curiously eyed the travelers in the low valley. Even from a distance, he saw the beautiful bronze armor reflecting the moonlight's silver hue. Next to the travelers' campsite were two fine horses. He rubbed his chin in thought, then quietly left in the darkness.

CHAPTER FIFTEEN

Before Apollo could even mount his sun chariot, Halcyon was yanked out of her bedroll by hands that were callused like her own. She stumbled and nearly toppled in the darkness, but she briefly saw two dirty faces pass hers. She was thrown onto her knees just as Cesare's yells filled her ears. A rusty iron blade tip pressed into her lower neck and stilled her.

"What is a freewoman doing traveling with a slave?" a bandit asked.

Halcyon cast a glance to Cesare, who was held at dagger point by two other men. Altogether she was dealing with four bandits, who probably considered these lands their territory. She returned her dark stare to the speaking bandit, glaring along the length of his ugly sword to his marred features above her. "We are headed to Corinth... to see family."

The bandit weighed the answer, then huffed low and indicated the armor to their side. "Yours?"

Halcyon ground her teeth and drew her fingers nearer the hidden dagger's hilt at her waist. She only had a slim chance to save herself and Cesare. Her heart lurched at dying out here by worthless bandits.

"It is hers," another bandit confirmed. The bandit had midnight hair, long strands braided behind his back, and wore a tattered leather cuirass. He was inspecting the armor that was beautifully crafted and confirmed it was indeed designed for a woman, not a man.

"A woman warrior," the leader bandit mocked, then flexed his grip on the sword hilt.

"These markings are of the hippeis," the dark-haired bandit further revealed. He dragged his fingertips along the stamp engraved at the right shoulder. His two comrades who held Cesare captive started talking low. He stood up and suggested, "Sciron, she could be worth a nice ransom."

The leader, Sciron, smiled toothily at the prospect of making more drachmas. "Iros, tie her." He kept his sword trained on Halcyon.

The dark-haired bandit, Iros, moved away from the armor. He reached behind his back and unhooked a length of coiled rope. He cautiously went behind Halcyon, nervous and cautious now that he knew she was more than just armor. He knelt down, then took her right wrist first. For a heartbeat, Iros thought it would go smoothly. But when he reached for her other wrist, a flash of bronze was faster than his holler of warning.

Halcyon tore the dagger free from the sheath at her hip, grazing her own flesh against the tip of the leader's sword in the process. The twinge of sharpness against her skin fueled her as she spun to her left and swung her dagger up. With deadly skill, Halcyon drove the dagger into Iros's neck, and blood poured from the wound. The bandit's dying gurgles were music to her.

Sciron was awestruck by Halcyon's skill, but he recovered and lunged at her. He missed and blew past her. He turned with the sword pointed at her. His body blocked Halcyon from obtaining her xiphos. Halcyon had her hands raised and bloody dagger at the ready. She backed up and stepped around the dead bandit.

Sciron bared his teeth then ordered, "Kill the slave, Pratinos." He made a bet and hoped he'd won it.

Pratinos was on Cesare's left, and he drew the blade tight against his neck. Cesare's initial scream made him slow down, but Pratinos only stopped cutting through the skin when Halcyon yelled at him.

"Stop!" Halcyon crumbled under the threat to Cesare's life. She tossed the bloody dagger to the ground and freely surrendered to the bandits, gritting her teeth.

Sciron smiled his yellow, broken teeth at the wealthy hoplite. Suddenly, his smile turned into a sneer, and he jumped forward with the blade overhead. He slammed his fist into Halcyon's jaw and took her down to her knees. Sciron jammed his right knee into Halcyon's chest, which threw her onto her back.

Halcyon groaned heavily, and dizziness swept through her head. A thread of panic charged through her when Sciron drew back his foot. She hastily covered her stomach with her arms before he kicked at her. Halcyon whimpered at the bolt of pain, but her arms took the brunt of it. She saw Sciron prepare to kick again, and she cringed at what it would do to the life forming in her belly.

"Please!" Cesare tried moving, but Pratinos tightened the blade to Cesare's throat. "She has suffered enough." He feared for Halcyon's developing baby in the womb.

Sciron growled low. "Hardly — compared to my dead friend." He returned his ire to the fallen hoplite. Murder shined in his eyes, even if he knew Halcyon's value as a ransom. His ragged breaths matched his rage. With a raised sword, Sciron hungered to cut into the woman's defiance.

Halcyon warred with her weakened body. She demanded her muscles to lift her and fight back, but she could barely sit up. All her attention was drawn to the rusty blade that reflected the moonlight. For the first time in her life, Halcyon felt true fear. It was for the unborn life in her belly, her instincts telling her to protect life. She frantically pleaded with the goddess Rhea, her first prayer to the Mother of the gods.

From the twinkling skies, Rhea listened to a mortal's appeal for motherhood, and she responded with thunder across the valleys. Her beautiful voice came out in a powerful yell and rolled through the campsite. A single word in a strange tongue to the Greek ear. Then a golden bolt cut through the darkness and collided with Sciron.

Halcyon gasped after Sciron fell to the ground beside her. She tingled with hints of strength and peered over her shoulder at the downed bandit. Even in the dark night, Halcyon made out the golden strands of her savior. "Thora," she whispered in awe. Like Halcyon, the two bandits beside Cesare were dumbstruck by Thora's arrival as if she were a goddess.

Quick to recover, Halcyon crawled over to her bloody dagger and fingered the hilt. She stole a concerned glance at Thora, who remained on top of Sciron's back.

Thora was several hands taller, bulkier than Sciron, and empowered by her raw anger. She hissed between clenched teeth and suddenly rolled them so that he was on top. Sciron was shocked by the action, barely registering the new position and saw his attacker flick something past his face. He only understood why when a rope noosed around his neck. Sciron choked and clawed at the thick coil across his throat while the stars twinkled above him.

At the same time, Halcyon dragged her fingertips down to the blade's tip and snared it. She rolled onto her back with her right arm retracted. In a heartbeat, she aligned her aim and threw the dagger at Cesare's captor. Pratinos screamed when the blade plunged into his right eye. He dropped his own dagger from the slave's throat.

The last bandit, Tros, watched his comrade fall to death and hastily backed away from Cesare. He had no weapons beyond his rough fists. Tros glanced at his leader, who was choking to death. He decided his life was more valuable than his leader's own and bolted from the campsite in fear.

Halcyon watched the bandit flee, then she turned her attention to Thora and Sciron. She flinched at the sudden silence in the camp. Sciron was limp against Thora and his eyes wide open toward the gods above them.

Thora removed the rope from around the bandit's neck. She shoved the dead body off and hurried to her feet. After a visual scan of the campsite, she went to her owner's side. "Halcyon," she whispered. There was strain in her voice from worry and fear.

For the first time, Halcyon heard her name on Thora's lips, and it settled warmly in her chest. She barely sat up when the Norsk slave knelt beside her. She sighed after concerned hands touched her, inspecting her for injury.

Cesare appeared on the other side of Halcyon. "Are you hurt, ĕra?"

Halcyon flinched from Cesare's gentle touch against her face. "I am fine." From her knelt position, she saw the thin line of blood on Cesare's neck from the bandit's blade. She gingerly lifted up until she was standing between the two slaves. Thora's hand was against her lower back. Gradually, Halcyon lifted her gaze until her eyes locked on Thora. For several silent moments, they exchanged emotions unspoken since they had parted ways.

"I will remove the bodies," Cesare said and planned to clean his wound. He itched to have space from the two warring women. His plan slightly failed when Thora assisted him.

Halcyon allowed it and, instead, tasked herself with starting a new fire. The chore's ease gave her a chance to absorb that Thora was here. Only shortly ago, Halcyon had been sleeping fitfully, and then her world was turned into chaos when the bandits arrived in their camp. Before the God of Death could find Halcyon, Thora had stormed into the campsite and saved her.

After the bodies were removed, the slaves sat around the campfire in tense silence. Nobody dared to speak first, because it was Halcyon's right as their owner. With a wary glance, Cesare confirmed that Halcyon was trying to grasp the recent events. Like Thora, he patiently waited to see what she would say.

Surprisingly, it was gratitude first from Halcyon. "Thank you for..." Halcyon gazed in the direction of the dead bandits. "For saving me."

"*Ekki at pakka*," Thora politely replied in her native tongue. She sat opposite of Halcyon on a rock and had a small pack leaning against it. Her few meager travel items were contained within the rucksack. Her features were deceivingly calm, but her stomach was wound tighter. Earlier she had been full of fire and wrath when the bandit was beating Halcyon.

"Ĕra," Cesare said cautiously, "I will gather more firewood."

Halcyon silently thanked Cesare's discretion. She indicated the hatchet beside the saddlebags. Once Cesare's footfall faded, she looked pointedly at Thora. "Why?"

Thora sat stiffly and uncomfortable with her current situation. There were so many answers to Halcyon's question, but each one ended the same way. She sighed. "You."

Halcyon dragged her teeth across her bottom lip. She nearly squirmed under the answer, but she was a gods damn hoplite, hardly a child.

"I am Norsk," Thora said. She lifted her gaze and lined her stormy blue eyes on Halcyon. "Norsk are not owned. We are not bought or controlled." Every flicker from the campfire was alive in her eyes. She thought back to the other night when she argued with Halcyon. The disagreement reminded her of her new place in the world and that Halcyon still saw her as property. "I will not be a slave... not even to you." She huffed low and stared into the fire. "I will die free and unbound, here or in my homelands."

Halcyon sat quietly and listened to Thora's beliefs. She related to them because, even as a freewoman, she was bound and enslaved until she put on the helmet. Under the bronze, she was a hoplite and a warrior among her people, no longer a woman enslaved by laws and social standards. In truth, Halcyon sadly admitted even as a hoplite, she had duties.

Thora knew that Halcyon understood her reasoning. It was only a question to delay the future. Halcyon had left the safety of her home and city in hopes to change the truth and retrieve Thora. Yet they both knew that Thora was free in spirit and would fight to be free in body. For now, Thora allowed Halcyon the fantasy that they could still sit as slave and owner, just a little longer.

With a slow reach, Halcyon fished out the tattered, handwritten message that Thora had left her. Yarikh had already translated the apology on one side, but she had no idea what was on the other. She unfolded the cloth and held that side out toward Thora.

After a deep breath, Thora translated the Norsk letters. "The wolf and the dog do not play together." She shifted on the hard, cool seat. "It is an old..." She attempted searching for the word in Greek.

"Saying," Halcyon provided.

"*Já*. It is an old saying with my people."

Halcyon fell silent and analyzed who was the wolf and who was the dog. She decided both were true in either case. After a heavy silence, she finally said, "You are right."

A thickness of sincerity was in Halcyon's voice that left Thora curious.

"I purchased you not to keep you," Halcyon said. Memories from months ago, of those first moments when she and Thora crossed lives, caused a warmth in her chest. "I purchased you to free you one day." A thin smile pulled against her lips when Thora stared at her in awe.

Thora opened her mouth slightly, but she was at a loss. She thought about Halcyon's plan, and tiny details started connecting in Thora's mind.

Unlike most Spartan homes, Halcyon purchased and owned her own slaves rather than using the helots from the polis. Such lifestyle as a personal slave protected Thora from threats by the government and other Spartans, especially the Crypteia. Yarikh's arrival and teachings were another progressive step toward Thora's freedom. Without the Greek tongue, Thora would indefinitely remain a barbarian among the Greeks. Smaller pieces were Thora's growing authority in the household and ability to shop in the agora, which was often done by male slaves. What had seemed like normal duties in Norsk culture were a show of authority or freedom in Sparta.

"But—" Halcyon paused as Thora refocused on her. "I cannot give you your freedom here." She indicated the wide open spaces of the rolling lands. "Only in Sparta before the polis."

Thora pursed her lips as she weighed her options to return to Sparta with Halcyon and Cesare. She considered whether her official freedom truly mattered to her. Even if she received it, she doubted it cleared her passage back to her people.

Halcyon was reading Thora's thoughts. She sighed heavily and offered, "If you wish then to return to your people, I will give you the supplies." She narrowed her gaze at Thora. "But you most likely will die or be enslaved again, Norsk or not." She said nothing else because Cesare had returned with an armload.

Thora broke from her thoughts and retrieved the second armload. When she returned, she found the campfire rekindled with fresh wood. Cesare was busy preparing a light meal. With a glance to the east, she realized daybreak was upon them. Normally at such a time, Thora would seek out a safe location and rest during the day. At night, she traveled through the lands in hopes nobody would see her. It was by sheer luck that she had come upon Halcyon's campsite, as if the gods willed it. Thora was just uncertain whether it was her gods or Halcyon's gods. Perhaps the Fates were one and the same in both religions.

After the morning meal, Halcyon began tacking her horse with Cesare's help. She still ached in certain spots after the bandits' attack but suspected the minor pains would be gone tomorrow. She left her horse hitched to a tree branch and allowed Cesare to prepare his own horse.

Eventually, Halcyon found her way to the dead bandits. She knelt by the leader and considered what little he had on him, but she was purely interested in his sword. She stripped the tattered leather sheath from Sciron. Halcyon then sheathed the rusty blade and left the dead to rot or be eaten by the wildlife. Perhaps the surviving bandit would return to bury his comrades.

In camp, Thora continued sitting by the fire, lost in thought and worry. Halcyon approached her and held out the sheathed blade. "This is now yours."

Thora curiously eyed Halcyon and took the weapon into her lap. Somehow the weathered sheath and ratty blade were worth more than all her meager food supplies. She had killed a man to earn it. And yet, Halcyon's life was priceless to her.

Halcyon offered nothing else and went to her horse. She freed the reins and took a steady breath before lifting herself onto the saddle. She waited until Cesare had done the same on his smaller horse. With a click of her tongue, she and Cesare rode southwest toward Sparta, toward home. Even if Thora had her freedom, legally or forced, it was a freedom not granted to Halcyon.

She was bound to her duty as a Spartan hoplite. She had to let go of Thora.

Thora continued running her fingers down the sheath's length. It had been nearly four years since she last held and owned a blade. Somehow the short Greek sword anchored her to the reality that she could have a life again. Gingerly, she pulled on the handle and sadly smiled at the rusty blade that peered out from the sheath. After she pushed it back in, she stood up and left the abandoned campsite.

In front of Thora, a shadow formed at her feet and stretched ahead of her. Her shadow guided her in the right direction, to freedom.

ᛖᛈᛁᛚᛟᚷᚢᛖ

With finality, the Spartan sealstone pressed into the wax at the bottom of a hand-scribed parchment paper. Slowly, it rocked deeper, and the hot wax hungrily spread through the stone's artistic lines. As the warm stone drew away, the wax cooled and revealed its wonder. A Spartan hoplite was driving his blade into his enemy's chest, and the lambda symbol was proudly etched in his aspis. The seal officially bound the document in the eyes of the polis as it unbound one woman from slavery.

"It is done." Dromeus set his sealstone to the side of his table, then held out the parchment. For many years, the council elder had known Halcyon. Before then, he'd known her mother.

Halcyon retrieved the document and nodded at Dromeus. "Thank you."

Dromeus studied the famed hoplite that stood over his desk. "What will she do now, Halcyon?"

With a soft shake of her head, Halcyon honestly replied, "I do not know."

Dromeus considered Halcyon for a moment. Several days ago, the first wave of fallen hoplites returned to Sparta from the war against Xerxes. Halcyon was one of the wives to receive her husband's lifeless, bloody body on top of his aspis. All the wives followed the proper rituals. A coin under the dead's tongue, body washed and anointed, and finally prayers before the burial. Dromeus recalled Halcyon's strength that day at the burial. There were no tears. Now, Dromeus wondered how she would manage a fatherless newborn.

Halcyon shifted under Dromeus's stern gaze. She halted his next attempt to further question her by saying goodbye to the councilman. Quietly, she left the building and found Cesare waiting for her on the street.

"Home, ěra?"

After a nod, Halcyon headed for her house set across the city. The autumn equinox had passed over a month ago. The day's cooler temperature offered relief from the summer's earlier swelter. Halcyon had made promises and was now fulfilling them. As she grew closer to the latched gate of her home, she felt her stomach pitch, then roll. Her damp fingers nearly dropped the sealed parchment.

Cesare pushed ahead, unlatched the gate, and held it open until Halcyon entered the courtyard. He closed the gate and quietly went about his chores.

Halcyon neared the kitchen and noted that Glauce was busy preparing for the day's last meal. She swept through the house but never found the target of her interest. After a little thought, Halcyon went to the second most likely spot. Next to the home, the small stable held three horses and three more empty stalls.

In the last stall, a tall, sunny-haired beauty continued brushing the white mare. Cheimon happily received the attention and thanked the human with a nudge. A loving pat to Cheimon's neck signaled the end of the brushing session.

"Thora," Halcyon said gently.

Thora returned the brush and left the stall, then met Halcyon halfway in the stable.

"Come with me." Halcyon guided her slave to a wooden bench near the stable. She often practiced in the open space, but today it was different. They sat facing the field far behind her home. For a moment, Halcyon watched the helots working hard in the field.

Thora followed her owner's gaze and considered the uglier life that she most likely had missed because Halcyon purchased her. She tore her gaze away and focused on her owner.

Halcyon retrieved the document and held it out, delicately. "This is yours." She had no idea how the document would change everything, especially for herself.

Thora grew excited at the power in the document. She unfolded it and attempted reading what she could, because her reading skills were still meager. The most important words burned into her mind and were sealed by the artistic wax symbol at the bottom. She ran her fingertips across the wax seal to ensure it was real. Each bump and dip unshackled her from her life as a slave.

"I am a freedwoman," Thora whispered.

Halcyon bowed her head and said, "You are no longer mine." Her voice cracked, and the storminess was clear in her eyes.

Such truthful words lifted Thora's ice blue eyes to her former owner.

Halcyon shifted on the bench and assumed her calm composure that her hoplite mentors had drilled into her over the years. "At first light, you are welcome to leave here. I will provide you with anything you require."

Thora's features softened at the kind offer. Halcyon may have been an irritable owner, but she was still generous in her own right. She slightly dipped her head, then cautiously asked, "And if I wish to stay?"

Halcyon slightly parted her lips, but nothing was forthcoming. Thora's question was sharper than a dory, cutting through her armor and flesh until it pierced her heart.

Thora eased Halcyon's discomfort with a soft touch to the knee. "I miss my people and my homelands, but... this is home." She searched the green eyes that studied her. "You are family to me."

Halcyon released a low, strained breath after the unlikely confession. Nearly a month ago, she had searched for Thora across the countryside. Perhaps it was to save Thora from re-enslavement or even death. Perhaps she wanted to drag Thora home. All those ideas died when she realized Thora was ready to be free. Halcyon had promised she would free Thora, if they returned to Sparta where it could be done. Today her promise was complete.

Halcyon remembered that Thora had been unsure about following Halcyon back to Sparta where her bonds awaited her. But Thora trusted her word, and they were always drawn to each other. Thora not only returned with her but also to a demolished owner and slave relationship. The destructive storm between them had left emotional debris. Day by day, they cleaned up the pieces until an unsuspecting friendship replaced the previous relationship.

All the remolding of their bond softly came from new routine and, later, common ground. Thora continued her usual daily routines around the home, upon Halcyon's request. Glauce and Cesare easily followed Thora's leadership. And Gorgo no longer came to the house.

Then one day, Halcyon offered to show Thora how to remove the rust from Thora's blade. Under Halcyon's instructions, Thora renewed the rusty xiphos until her blue eyes were reflected in the blade. A few days later, she schooled Thora on how to hold the short sword, along with a few slashing techniques. Eventually, sword lessons became a nearly daily event in the late afternoons, and she secretly respected Thora's natural skill with the blade.

"Halcyon?" Thora asked softly. She watched the memories fade from Halcyon's features.

Slowly, Halcyon focused on Thora seated beside her. For only the second time, Thora had whispered her name, yet it made

Halcyon's heart thunder. She saw the certainty in Thora's features that this was now home. "Stay," she replied tenderly after covering Thora's hand. She imagined a full life shared with Thora and even her future child. Bitterness about the pregnancy no longer gripped her heart, especially with Thora at her side.

Halcyon's whisper flooded Thora's chest and washed away the last doubtful fragments. Thora smiled, in relief and happiness. Halcyon's feather-light touch to her flushed cheek drew Thora's head down, closer. At first, Thora held her breath until Halcyon's lips brushed across hers. A wild bolt cut through her stomach and made Thora moan.

Sliding her hand behind Thora's neck, Halcyon gently pulled until their lips finally sealed together. She returned the moan when their mouths parted for the first time. Emotions danced between the soft caresses of their tongues. All the difficulties had led to this moment. And all the fears that Thora's freedom meant loneliness for Halcyon were gone.

As Thora drew back, she ached at seeing the salty droplets that fell from Halcyon's eyes. Like Halcyon, she trembled at both the excitement and the unknown ahead of them. There was much to be discussed, but it was less important than their closeness. Thora leaned down again and grazed her nose across Halcyon's own. She rekindled their earlier kiss, slow and tender.

What Thora once had in her homelands was a memory. Her family had been torn apart, and her husband dined with the gods. Norsk war and strife had enslaved her, but it was Greece that unbound her from the past. And Halcyon had unexpectedly become her home. Together, they found freedom in each other.

THE END

Glossary of Terms

Note: Terms listed alphabetically.

Agora: Originally an open assembly location in the town for political meetings, but later added a market where merchants sold their goods. In Sparta, commerce was discouraged by the government but supplies, materials, and wares were still necessary for daily life. Typically male helots and slaves went to the *agora* to minimize outside ideas and news from passing onto the Spartan citizens.

Andron: The portion of the house solely reserved for only the men, especially the husband. Typically political functions were held in the *andron* by the husband, and the nicest décor was located in the *andron*.

Aspis: A three-foot-diameter wooden shield carried by hoplites. The *aspis* allowed for hoplites to cross rivers since it was made of wood. Its concave structure also made it easier to move bodies after battle. In Spartan culture, the *aspis* was bronze coated with the symbol for Lambda upon it. It was the highest regarded weapon and to lose it was a disgrace.

Bouleuterion: A building where the council of citizens (*boule*) met during ancient times. Often it was located near the *agora*.

Chiton: An article of clothing worn by both men and women in Ancient Greece. The *chiton* was single piece of linen or wool fabric that was draped over the body, pinned at the shoulders, and a belt was worn across the waist or hips.

Chlamys: A short piece of cloak usually made from wool.

Chous: A transport jug for holding wine often found in the *agora*. The plural form is *choes*.

Dory: A six to ten-foot-long spear that also had a "spike" butt end for counterbalance. The *dory* was a hoplite's main weapon and was often used to stab at the enemy. However, it was rarely thrown like a javelin.

Drachma(s): Ancient Greek currency that literally translates to "to grasp." The *drachma* was used throughout all the Greek city-states, except for Sparta.

Ěra: A title that translates to the "lady of the house" in relation to her slaves. Only slaves called their female owners *ěra*.

Ěrus: A title that translates to the "lord." Only slaves called their male owners *ěrus* or *ěre*.

Exomis: A piece of Greek attire similar to a tunic that left the right arm and shoulder uncovered for optimal fighting.

Gastrin: A traditional dessert in Ancient Greece that is similar to baklava that originated in Crete. The pastry was made from several layers of dough that included sesame seeds, pepper, and poppy seeds then sweetened with *petimezi* (grape sugar).

Girdle: A thin belt worn by both men and women in Ancient Greece.

Gynaikeion: A portion of the home or a building especially reserved for only the women, including the wife. The room(s) or building tended to be remote and away from the public eye.

Helot: A lower class of serfs in Sparta, often considered slaves. They handled daily chores, farmed, and were tradesmen, allowing for Spartan citizens to focus on training, war, and politics.

Heraea Games: An ancient athletic competition similar to the Olympics that was sanctioned for women. However, women had to wear *chitons* during the competition unlike men, who competed in the nude.

Hippeus: A wealthy cavalryman of the Greek army that had the money to afford a warhorse. More than one cavalryman was known as *hippeis*. However, in classical Sparta, a *hippeus* did not ride a horse and remained on foot as regular military. A Spartan *hippeus* was distinguished from other hoplites by the fact they were chosen and assigned to a Spartan king as the royal guard. Often three hundred *hippeis* swore loyalty to the king.

Kalamos: An ancient writing instrument similar to the quill, but made from reed plants. A single piece of reed was cut to length and given a sharpened point to hold ink.

Kline: Ancient Greek furniture comparable to a modern-day sofa. It was often made from wood or bronze then a lavish mattress was added on top for the wealthy. The *kline* was typically used at dinner, and the person would eat lying across but in an upright position.

Oinochoe: Literally translates to "I pour" in Greek. It is a wine jug or pitcher commonly used around the Greek home. There were eight styles in Ancient Greece. Most *oinochoe* were decorated or undecorated and came in clay or metal.

Ouranē: Ancient Greek chamber pot.

Pais: The Greek word for young male lover.

Peplos: A full length of robe-style cloth only worn by Greek women. It was often rectangular in design and hung from the shoulders then folded vertically. Typically it was worn with a belt.

Polis: A polis translates to "city-state," which is the government, people, and citizenship in Ancient Greece. Plural version is *poleis*.

Skyphos: A two-handed cup made for wine. They were deep and often made from clay, but also from silver. *Skyphoi* is the plural version.

Symposium: A type of social party that literally translates to "to drink together." The party was hosted by aristocrats and meant for men so that they could converse, drink, debate, and be social.

Thalamus: The great bedroom of the master and mistress of the house. Often, but not always, the great bedroom opens to the courtyard. The finest furniture and ornaments are held within the great bedroom.

Triobol: A form of ancient Greek currency that equaled about half a drachma.

Xiphos: An iron forged sword about twenty to twenty-four inches long and double-edged. It was considered the hoplite's secondary weapon to the *dory*. Spartan hoplites were rumored to use a shorter *xiphos* about twelve inches long.

About the Author

Cameron North started creative writing at an early age as a teenager and always had a soft spot for strong female leads in books, comics, television, and movies. Later, she began sharing her work and dreamed of becoming an author. Eventually all her efforts with writing have brought her to publish LGBTQ+ books that are sci-fi, fantasy, historic, and romance in nature. Every book is full of heart and passion for both the characters and the plot, loving the journey each time.

Born in Maryland, Cameron enjoys the rural Eastern Shore and the Chesapeake Bay, especially boating on the rivers. She graduated with a business degree in Information Systems due to her love for computers and technology. Currently, Cameron works full-time and dedicates all her free-time to her writing and publishing. Her other hobbies include raising chickens, gardening, airplanes, and traveling abroad. Today, she continues to live on the Eastern Shore and sharing adventures with her wife, dog, cat, and flock of chickens.

To learn more about Cameron's published books, please visit WASP Publishing's website at www.WASPpublishing.com

Connect With the Author

All the ways to connect with Cameron North:

Website
www.WASPpublishing.com

Join the WASP Publishing Newsletter
https://www.WASPpublishing.com/newsletter

Email:
CameronLNorth@gmail.com